D0910993

Truth Be Told

Bonita Y. McCoy

Courageous Writers

Cover Design by Lucy Burton

Truth Be Told
© 2018 Bonita Y. McCoy

ISBN – 13-978-1-949208-01-6
ISBN*-13-978-1-949208-00-9 eBook:

All rights reserved. No part of this publication may be reproduced or transmitted in any form or by any means without written permission from the publisher.

Scripture quotations are from the Holy Bible, English Standard Version ® (ESV®), copyright© 2001 by Crossway, a publishing ministry of Good News Publishers. Used by permission. All rights reserved.

This book is a work of fiction. Names, characters, places, and incidents are either a product of the author's imagination or used fictitiously. Any similarity to actual people or events is purely coincidental.

Published by Courageous Writers, P.O. Box 292, Harvest, AL. 35749.

Printed in the United States of America

Cover Design by Lucy Burton

Dedicated to:
My Aunt Jeanne

Who taught me the truth of Jesus

I am the way, and the truth, and the life. No one comes to the Father except through me. John 14:6

Acknowledgements

Stories are never plotted, wrestled into submission, or pushed forward without the help of many others, so my thanks goes out to all these wonderful individuals and groups who helped me keep my eye on the goal.

My hubby and number one patron of the arts is responsible for me writing at all. My sons (all of them) and their patience over the years as I typed away at the keyboard, even close to dinner time, needs to be mentioned.

Family, friends and prayer partners who kept me encouraged, lifted up, and moving in the right direction always pointing me to Jesus – Margaret and the Jesus Girls.

Thanks goes to my plotting friend Gretchen, without her, some of the humor would've been lost and a lot of the action would've been stiff. Love your sense of fun.

My critique partner and all the Beta Readers whose input formed and reformed many of the scenes in this book. And all the Super Henrys out there who inspire us!!

Thank You!!

God's Blessings
Bonita

Chapter One

Claire tightened her fingers around the steering wheel turning her knuckles white.

The end of another job. She swallowed the lump in her throat as she struggled to keep the hot tears at bay. Was this the fourth or fifth one since she and Henry moved to Alabama last spring?

Her old truck rattled in protest as she pushed hard against the gas pedal. Staring out the windshield unseeing, she allowed herself to ping-pong between anger and self-pity.

The tires of her 1995 Dodge pick-up spit out the dirt as she ate up the distance between her rental house and Main Street.

She had left Florida, needing a fresh start and landed in Miller Creek, Alabama. Now, she couldn't count the number of fresh starts she'd had.

Where had the year gone? Claire hit the gas harder. The warm April wind whipped through the open windows and blew her brown shoulder length hair into her eyes. She struggled to push it out of the way, but she didn't slow down. The truck began to sputter. Nothing new. It needed repairs. Everything needed repairs. Her truck, her finances, her life.

She turned off the dirt road onto the highway and drove another five minutes before turning onto Main Street. Her destination – Adele's Café. The home of the best double bacon cheeseburger she had ever put in her mouth. She could almost smell the bacon. Comfort food at its finest, and boy, how she needed it today.

Signing the divorce papers last year had left Claire and Henry on their own. The death of a family. Something that couldn't be repaired.

He had said forever, what he meant was until. Claire shook the thought away in time to see the tail lights of the truck in front of her flash red.

She slammed on the brakes. Frustration boiled up inside her.

The driver of the offending truck called, "Hey Haden," out his open window. A tall man, coming out of Adele's Café, strolled over and leaned his forearms against the passenger side window. She recognized him as one of the owners of Sawyer Construction. She didn't know him personally, but his Aunt Adele talked about him often.

"Come on, already." The impulse to honk surged through her, but she knew it'd do no good. The horn didn't work.

Haden Sawyer seemed in no hurry to free up traffic. He shifted from one leg to the other as he talked, not once looking her way.

That's the problem with living in small town Mayberry. People think it's normal to conduct business in the middle of the street. Claire checked her watch out of habit. What did it matter? She didn't have anywhere to be, no job, no time crunch.

Fed up with waiting, she threw the truck into reverse, but to her annoyance, someone had pulled up behind her.

Stuck, she leaned over to her passenger side window. Pulling against the seat belt, she strained to get as close to the window as possible. "Hey!" She yelled.

No response.

She got louder. "Hey, move it already!"

Haden turned his head and held up his hand to show he had heard her but didn't budge. The driver must've said something funny because he grinned giving Claire a clear view of his dimples.

The fact she noticed how good looking he was irritated her. Cute, homely, who cares? Men. Inconsiderate men. They hire you; they fire you. They cause traffic jams.

Claire sat up, unclicked her seat belt, and shoved open the door. "What do you think you're doing?"

"See ya, Charlie." As the truck pulled away, Haden turned to leave.

"Don't walk away from me." Claire sprinted to catch him before he hit the sidewalk. She grabbed his arm, dragging him to a halt.

"Answer me. What were you doing holding up traffic? I hope it was *really* important."

"Look, I stopped to talk to someone about an upcoming event. No one was behind him when he stopped, and it didn't take long. It's no big deal."

"I was behind him when he stopped. What if everybody held their conversations in the middle of the street like you? Imagine the wrecks, the chaos." Claire stood on her tiptoes, trying to meet the guy's eyes. Even with her boots and their two-inch heels, she didn't come close

"I imagine it would look something like that," he nodded towards the street.

Claire turned to find three cars stacked behind her old truck. With one on the other side of the road stopped by the open door. No one honked; instead, they watched. Free entertainment.

"Great, just great." Claire ran for her truck and jumped in. "You know this is your fault, right?" She yelled out the window.

"Lady," said Haden as he backed up to the curb. "I'm not the one parked in the street."

Claire revved her engine as she watched Haden saunter off down the sidewalk. One of the three cars behind her laid on the horn. She threw the sputtering truck into drive and pulled into the empty parking space outside of Adele's Café, now available since the other truck had moved.

Men.

∞

Adele's Café held a certain charm. It hadn't aged a day past the 1950's. To the left of the entrance, ran four rows of booths the length of the café. The seats were red vinyl, and the tables were covered with red checkered table clothes. In the middle of each table, sat a small vase full of fresh flowers.

To the right of the entrance sat an old fashion soda fountain counter, with swivel stools and a foot rest that ran its length. The counter curved at one end. The wall behind it sported posters, school pendants, awards, photos, and other pieces of the history of the café and its owner.

Adele, a slightly plump woman who never met a stranger, listened to Claire Reed repeat word for word the phone call she had received that morning. "What am I going to do?" Claire rested her chin in her hand. Her green eyes dimmed with worry. "I can't be unemployed. Henry's medical bills are piling up. If I keep losing jobs at this rate, I'll never get caught up."

"Oh, honey, it's going to be all right. You know the saying when God closes a door; he opens a window nearby." Adele pushed her short salt and pepper hair behind her ear and refilled Claire's mug before replacing the coffee pot on the burner.

"So far, he's closed three doors in the last eight months. Miller Creek isn't big enough for me to keep getting let go." Adele saw Claire's chin quiver. She fought the urge to wrap the younger woman in a hug. "And I don't see any windows flying open." Adele reached out and patted Claire's hand. Adele admired her spunk, but her heart ached for her and her son. Claire was so young, maybe twenty-eight, to be carrying such a heavy burden.

"Hey, Adele, am I getting those eggs today, or should I come back next week?" Sid called.

"Hold your horses. What's your rush? Are you afraid your new bride is going to run off like your old dog?" All the regulars laughed.

Sid, a cantankerous burr who couldn't even keep a pet, had let Adele play matchmaker for him. He'd never been happier.

"No, my old dog never appreciated my cooking the way Katie does." His grin crept across his face as he looked down at his boots. "I don't think she'll be running off nowhere. She says she couldn't survive without my strawberry short-cake."

Adele laughed. "I told you those culinary charms of yours would pay off."

Retrieving Sid's order from the pick-up window, she turned to Claire. "I'll be right back, dear. Don't leave."

Adele weaved her way in and out between the booths like a dancer performing familiar steps. In spite of her sturdy build and age, she moved with agility. Sixty wasn't that big of a deal. She deposited the order in front of Sid who stood at the cash register. "Bon appetit."

The bell on the door jingled letting Adele know she had another customer. She turned. "Good Morning and welcome to …" She stopped when she recognized her nephew, Jed. "Well, hello, stranger. I haven't seen you in a month of Sundays." Arms wide open, she pulled him into a bear hug.

"I know. We've been swamped. Haden has us working over-time trying to catch up." Jed groaned. "We have two projects that are behind schedule, and it didn't help any when Doris quit."

"Doris quit?" Adele pulled herself from his embrace to look up into his face.

"Yeah, this is the third one this year."

"Oh, that's terrible, but it explains some things."

"Haden's been wound so tight, all he does is bark out orders. He's been meaner than a bulldog."

"You can't blame him for putting up a wall. This last year's been tough."

"Maybe, but I'm about to knock it down for him if he's not careful." Jed shook his head.

"Well, take a seat at the counter, and I'll get Frank to whip you up some cheese grits. That ought to sooth your weary soul." Jed winked at her and moved toward an empty stool.

As Adele hurried behind the counter, she caught sight of Claire. Things began to churn in her mind. She leaned close to the window and yelled in the order. "One order of cheese grits, extra cheesy." But she didn't make eye contact with Frank, the cook. She kept her eyes on Claire.

Claire sat absorbed in the newspaper unaware she was being scrutinized. She had it opened to the help wanted section.

Adele picked up the coffee pot and a clean mug. She took three steps and planted herself in front of her nephew who sat two seats to the left of Claire.

As she poured the coffee, she raised her voice. “So, Doris quit. I guess you and Haden are looking for a replacement.” Here, she paused and stared at Claire until she looked up from her paper.

Adele nodded towards Jed.

∞

Claire followed Adele’s gaze. “Jed, this is Claire Reed. Claire, this is my nephew, Jed Sawyer. He’s looking for a secretary.”

“So, I heard.” Claire recognized Jed from around town.

“To be clear, the opening is for an administrative assistant, and you’d be working primarily with my brother, Haden.”

“Haden Sawyer?” Claire tensed. “Oh, I…well, I am looking for a position. But…Adele shouldn’t have said anything to you.” Claire picked up the paper and resumed her search, hoping Jed would take the hint.

“Why not? She’s right. We’re looking for a replacement, and someone with experience would be great.” Claire gave Jed a sideways glance. “You don’t happen to have any experience running an office, do you?”

Claire set her jaw as she closed the paper and pulled her purse from the stool beside her. “Yes, I do have experience, lots of experience, and to be frank, I could do the job in my sleep. But there’s a problem, and it’s the same one that’s cost me all my other jobs. I have a son.”

Claire whipped her purse onto her shoulder, stood, and marched towards the cash register. She heard Jed's boots hitting the tile as he rushed to catch up to her.

"Last I looked, having kids wasn't a crime."

Claire placed her purse on the counter and pushing aside envelopes and gum wrappers, dug out her wallet. "No but having to take time off for their medical condition seems to be."

"Oh, did you let them know in advance you'd need time off?"

Claire's fists tightened around her purse straps. "Gee, why didn't I think of that?" She smacked her forehead with the palm of her hand. "Oh yeah, I did."

Cherie, the red-haired waitress, made her way over to the register and punched in Claire's bill. "That'll be $6.53."

Claire opened the clasp on her wallet and handed her five, one-dollar bills.

"That's only five, sweetie."

"I know. Give me a minute. I've got some change." Claire dumped the remaining contents of her wallet onto the brown Formica counter top. The coins bounced against the hard surface, clinking and clanging. Claire slapped her hand on top of them, to keep them from jumping off onto the floor.

"Here let me help." Jed took a step towards her.

"No, no…I've got this." Claire began to count under her breath. She handed Cherie a dollar in quarters and continued. "Ten, fifteen, twenty-five, twenty-eight." Claire froze.

"Here, I've got a quarter." Jed produced the needed coin from his pocket.

Claire looked from the quarter in his hand, up to his face and back to the quarter. "Are you sure?" Claire swallowed the lump, forming in her throat. The heat of embarrassment colored her cheeks pink.

"It's a quarter. You can pay me back when you interview for the administrative assistant's position tomorrow." Jed handed her the quarter.

"Isn't that a twenty-five-cent word for secretary?" Claire held up the quarter, pinched between her thumb and pointer finger. Humor seemed appropriate.

Jed grinned, took a business card out of his jean pocket and wrote something on the back of it. "Here, be at the office at 10 o'clock. I'll let Haden know to expect you."

Claire turned the card over in her hand. "Sawyer Construction Company," she read. "dependable, reliable, building our name one job at a time." She paused and met Jed's eyes. "Loyal and dependable, huh? Well, we'll see about that."

She handed the coin to the waitress and scooped up the three pennies which remained on the counter.

"Have a good day, honey." Cherie called as she pushed the cash draw shut.

Claire muttered, "Yeah, we'll see about that too."

Chapter Two

Adele watched Jed saunter back to the stool. He grinned when he found his cheese grits waiting for him. She took in his antics as he inhaled the steam, waving it up towards his nose the way he had as a kid.

Adele finished clearing Claire's spot and drifted back behind the counter.

As she placed the empty mug and plate in the gray bin, she heard Jed clear his throat. "Alright, you little imp." Adele swirled around. She saw the dimples, playing at the corners of his mouth.

"Is that anyway to talk to your elder?" Adele propped her hand on her ample hip.

Jed raised his voice a little more. "Elder is right."

"Quit yelling! I'm not hard of hearing."

"Could've fooled me the way you yelled out about us needing help."

"Stop that! Right now," Adele's voice had gone from normal to a low raspy whisper. "You'll scare the customers."

Even louder, he called out, "Maybe we should invest in a hearing aid for you, Aunt Adele, after all you're practically…"

Before Jed could finish, Adele pushed the bowl of hot cheese grits into his lap.

"Jed Sawyer, you know better than to tell a woman's age. If you weren't a grown man, I'd turn you over my knee right this minute."

"I'll be glad to take care of that for you, Adele," Cherie winked at

Jed.

"Oh, now, don't go playing with my heart. You know how long it took me to get over you the last time." Jed fanned his shirt away from his body to cool the hot grits.

Cherie laughed. "If I was twenty years younger, but the lady you were jawing with at the cash register. Now, she's about the right age and cute too."

Adele threw Jed a towel, so he could clean up the pile in his lap. "Okay, you two don't go trying to use any of your matchmaking vibes on me. It's Haden you need to be working on. He's miserable ever since… Well, you know."

"Who said I wasn't thinking about Haden." Adele wiped the counter in front of Jed, pulling the scattered bits into her hand. "I think Claire Reed might be the cure for what is ailing him, a little breath of fresh air so to speak."

"You mean a swift kick in the pants, don't you?"

"Either way," Adele answered with a twinkle in her eye. "Claire's the one for the job."

Jed and Cherie both groaned. Adele waved away their unwelcome complaints.

"Aunt Adele, stick to the matchmaking and leave the puns to the professionals."

∞

Haden Sawyer's office sat in the back of a double-wide trailer. His father who owned the company for over thirty years loved the feel of the metal building. He said the trailer to him represented a working man's space.

For Haden, the old doublewide reminded him of family. It held memories of his childhood and growth into a man. Sometimes on cold days, he could still smell the apple scent of his father's cigar, wafting through the small space as the heater roared into action.

"Look, all I'm saying is give the woman a chance." It was nine-thirty, and Haden had been listening to Jed's begging for the last twenty minutes.

"I wish you would've at least given me the opportunity to find my own secretary. It's bad enough I inherited handling the majority of the paperwork after Dad died; can't I find my own help?"

"It's not my fault, little brother, if you're the one with the business degree. Besides, finding the help isn't the problem. It's keeping the help which eludes you. You keep running them off ever since… Well, you know. Besides, Kyle and I have to work with her too. We should have some say."

Haden slumped back in his leather chair and folded his hands across his midsection. His heavy boots clunked against the side of the desk. He knew his brother was right, but he didn't have to like it. "Okay, when will she be here?"

Jed looked down at his watch. Meeting Haden's waiting eyes, he said, "in about fifteen minutes."

Haden jumped up, knocking the chair out from under him to the floor. "You've got to be kidding."

"No, I told her to be here at ten."

Haden surveyed his surroundings.

Chinese take-out boxes, foam containers, and empty soda cans loitered on every surface in the room, including half of his desk. Paperwork either needing his attention or needing to be filed covered the other half. Even the computer lay three feet under.

"Chill, Haden, this is why you need an administrative assistant," said Jed.

"Can't you just call her a secretary?"

"I don't think that's politically correct."

Haden groaned. "I don't care if it's politically correct or not. I'm calling her a secretary."

"Fine, but when she protests and threatens to sue, don't come whining to me."

"Like I whine."

"Haden, I'm your brother. You whine, and," he paused to look around the room. "You're a slob."

The front door shut with a thud.

Haden moved toward the hall that led to the front of the trailer.

Jed grabbed his arm as he pasted and whispered, "Be nice. We need her."

"That's for me to decide." Haden pulled from Jed's grip and walked down the narrow hall. A desk, some filing cabinets, a couple of plastic chairs, and a small kitchen made up the reception area.

He stopped short when he recognized a rather well-formed brunette standing by the stove. She was frowning down at the black goo, which covered the burner. The wannabe traffic cop. Great.

Chapter Three

Haden steeled himself and moved further into the room. "You must be Claire Reed."

"Yes, and you're the guy from yesterday's traffic jam." A scowl appeared on her face.

"Guilty." Haden shifted his weight under Claire's scrutiny. "I should apologize for my remark. I know better..." Haden started.

Claire shook her head. "No, I'm the one who needs to apologize. I wasn't myself. I'd received some bad news."

"No apology necessary. I was acting like a jerk."

"Do you think we could start again?" She asked.

Relieved, he said, "I'm Haden Sawyer," and extended his hand. "Nice to meet you."

"You too. I'm Claire Reed." Haden took her hand, his larger one swallowing hers. The softness of her hand against his sent a jolt straight through him. Without meaning to, he jerked his hand out of hers.

Jed wandered into the room about that time. Haden shot him a look afraid he'd seen his reaction to Claire.

"Hi, how are you?" Claire greeted him with a smile.

"I'm great. Sure, glad you decided to come by."

"Well, I had to pay my debt, right?" Claire reached in her front pocket and pulled out a shiny new coin.

"Nice." Jed took it from her. Haden noticed Jed's fingers lingered as he touched Claire's hand. "Where's my interest?"

Claire's face lit up at Jed's teasing.

"Don't you have somewhere to be?" asked Haden.

"Yeah, I'm supposed to be down at the Thomas site. We've got the foundation poured and need to start the framing."

"Sounds interesting." Claire beamed.

"Then you better head down there," said Haden. "And we'll go do this interview. Like you asked."

"Great," said Jed, but his feet didn't move.

"Claire, why don't we go back to my office? It's down this way." Haden pointed to the hall.

"Sure." She crossed the room and disappeared down the hallway.

Haden followed but stopped short. He turned to Jed and pointed towards the door. "You can leave now."

Jed put both hands up in surrender, "I'm going, but if I get a vote, we keep her. I don't care if you like it or not. We need somebody."

"Out!" he bellowed. When he turned around, he found Claire standing in the doorway of his office with her arms crossed, frowning at him like he was burnt goo.

∞

Haden grew more agitated as he hunted for the interview questions he had printed off the internet, four secretaries ago. He was keenly aware of Claire, who stood, waiting as he searched.

Lorraine had been with his Dad for over a decade, but after two years of training him, she retired. Who could blame her?

That's when he had needed the questions. The other secretaries had paraded through over the last year. Doris bringing up the rear. He had been full of hope for her.

Once Haden located the necessary piece of paper, he leaned over and picked up his chair, setting it straight before offering a chair to Claire.

"Have a seat, please." Haden pointed to an empty surface facing him.

"Is this how you normally keep your office?" asked Claire as she dusted off the seat.

"Only when I'm on my own. Now, Claire, why are you interested in this position?"

"I'm not," she stated. "I mean, I didn't know about the position until yesterday when your Aunt Adele and Jed told me about it. And up until then, I was employed."

"Oh, okay," Haden scanned the sheet of questions. "why do you want to work for our company?"

"I just told you. I'm unemployed." Claire scowled. The corners of her mouth pulling taunt.

"Yes, but why do you think you'd make a good secretary." Haden tensed, expecting there to be back lash from the word. After Jed's comments, he half expected her to storm out. Claire didn't flinch.

"I've done administrative work before, everything from filing to managing others. I also have a degree in business which means I know some of the terminology on contracts and such. Do you and Jed fight often?"

Haden looked up from the notes he was taking. Her vibrant green eyes met his. His stomach did a weird jiggle thing, and he touched it. "No, not often. We tend to work well together."

"Who all works here?"

"There's myself, Jed, and our cousin, Kyle. We run things. My Dad left the company to the three of us. We also have a couple of foremen and several workers who are on our payroll."

"Will I be interacting with them on a regular basis?"

"Yes, they're in and out picking up materials or putting in orders or finding out about subcontractors." Haden leaned back in his chair. "I thought I was interviewing you."

"That may be true, but it's obvious you didn't want to interview me. I mean after what happened out there." Claire motioned over her shoulder towards the other room. "Then you've got those cliché questions. I bet you found them on the internet."

Haden frowned.

"See if this sounds right 'What are your greatest strengths? List your weaknesses, where do you see yourself in five years, what makes you the best fit for the job?'"

"No wonder you're unemployed. Do you always go around sabotaging your interviews or just this one?" This slipped out before Haden could check himself.

"Just this one," Claire grabbed her purse from off the floor. "This was a mistake. From what Jed said yesterday, I thought you wanted someone." She stood.

"I do want someone. Look around you. We need help." Haden stood, his voice growing louder. "It doesn't take a genius to figure out we're drowning."

"If you need my help, then why are you yelling at me." The color rose in Claire's cheeks.

Haden froze.

He cleared his throat. "I'm sorry Claire. If you would, could we finish this interview. Jed thought you'd be great for the job, so I want to give this a fair chance." Haden sat down, turning the sheet of interview questions over and putting them aside.

"So, you admit you didn't want to take this interview." Claire cocked her head to one side. Her brown hair cascaded to her shoulder.

"I admit it, but from what you said, you're more than qualified. So, why don't I ask you the real question I need answered."

"Okay." Claire took her seat. "What do you want to know?"

"Why are you unemployed?"

Claire played with the strap on her purse. "Because I have a son."

Haden wasn't sure he had heard her right. "What do you mean because you have a son. Lots of women who work have families."

"Yes, but my son has a medical condition which requires me to take time off for his infusions. He also has a list of specialists he needs to see for routine maintenance. At least, that's what they call it."

"How old is your son?"

Claire smiled. "You're the first person in a while to ask about Henry as a kid not a pin cushion."

"Oh, his name is Henry. That was my grandfather's name." Haden leaned his forearms on his desk.

"Well, what do you know, common ground," said Claire. Haden smiled and watched as a mischievous twinkle crept into her eyes. He could get lost in those eyes. Claire continued without looking away, "Henry is five. He has an autoimmune disease called Juvenile Myositis."

"I take it you informed your other employers about his condition. What happened?"

"They were all very sympathetic until reality set in. When it did, they were as equally apologetic for having to let me go."

"Does his father have this same problem. I mean I'm sure he wants to be there when you and Henry need him."

Claire looked down at her hands. "Henry's dad left right after he was diagnosed. We're divorced. Henry doesn't remember him."

Haden's heart melted. He knew his own pain from the loss of his father. He hated to think what it would be like for Henry knowing his father had chosen to leave. He couldn't help but wonder what kind of a man deserts his family when they needed him the most.

Haden felt about two inches tall. Why had he acted so petty with Claire? So, interviewing her was like walking through molasses, big deal.

"Okay, so let's talk reality. What kind of flexibility do you need? I mean I'll need to know so I can present a clear picture to Kyle and Jed. I'll have to tell them about Henry's condition. Is that okay?"

Claire placed her purse on the floor before leaning back in the chair. Haden saw her shoulders relax. His asking permission must have touched on something.

"Of course. If you're serious, the best flexibility is to let me set my own schedule as long as I get the forty hours in each week. I know it's not possible, but it is what would work best for me."

"You're right. That would be hard for us to do. We need someone here when we're here." Haden slumped back and laced his fingers together across his midsection. "Would flexible hours between six and six help?"

"Yes, it would." Claire's smile spread from her lips to her eyes. Haden hated it, but he noticed her lips looked like the color of sweet summer strawberries.

∞

Claire noticed Haden had left the door open when they entered. She wondered if he was afraid to be alone with her. But then, she remembered the talk around town last year about Haden Sawyer and some girl. She didn't like listening to gossip, so the details had been lost on her.

"The flexible hours would be a god-send." She heard herself saying. "Between Henry's medical issues and him being a five-year-old boy, I have my hands full. I appreciate this."

"Glad to help." Haden's eyes never veered from her as they sat across from one another. She couldn't help feeling he was sizing her up. He had admitted he didn't want to be here interviewing her, but this seemed different, like he was measuring her more as a woman than as a potential employee.

"So, when do I start?"

Haden looked away. "Oh, uh…You see," he stammered. "I'll need to talk it over with Kyle and Jed. However, I should be able to let you know something tomorrow. Will that work for you?"

"Sure, that'll be fine." Claire's heart sank. She recognized the stall tactic. She had been on enough interviews in the last year, since the divorce had been final, to know how the game was played. Buy some time, see if anyone else applies, hire her as a last resort.

A sigh slipped from her lips.

"Claire, I will contact you tomorrow." She recognized genuine concern in Haden's brown eyes. "I'm not trying to put you off. Besides you heard Jed, he already voted to keep you. Heck, if you could cook, he might propose."

"Oh, good heavens no, I don't need a man in my life. It's already too complicated with my little guy. A big one would be overkill." Did she just say that out loud? To a handsome man, in the middle of an interview, for a job she needed? Heat crept up the back of her neck. She shuddered to think what kind of impression she was making on him.

To give herself time to recover, she bent over to pick up her purse.

When she looked up, Haden was standing, watching her. His smile accented by the dimples that creased his cheeks. "I must admit this has been the most unique interview I've ever held."

"It's not the worst I've had, but it does rank in the top three." Claire found herself grinning like a smitten school girl. "But I appreciate you using the word unique."

Haden chuckled and moved towards her. "Let me walk you to the door."

Claire rose from her seat, flustered. "Oh, that's not necessary." Claire tucked her black bag under her arm and headed for the open door.

She could smell his woodsy aroma as he followed close behind her, down the narrow hallway. He smelled like a forest after a rain and something else. She took in a deep breath.

"Are you okay?" Haden asked.

Claire turned, talking over her shoulder, "Fine."

The dimples made an encore appearance as Claire quickened her pace.

She needed to leave before he decided she was too incompetent to hire.

Haden took a deep breath himself. "Ooh, we've got to clean this place up."

"Well, that will be my first order of business…if you hire me." Claire reached for the doorknob and looked back at Haden. "Don't forget, tomorrow."

"I won't." He promised.

Claire left, expecting never to hear from the brown-eyed, dimpled devil of a construction worker, again.

Chapter Four

Henry, in his PJ's with his red cape hanging down his back, sat on his bed waiting for Claire to read to him. Claire loved this part of her day. She considered it the pay-off for being a mom. She viewed it as precious and guarded it from the nagging worries of bills and doctor appointments. This time belonged to them.

A large basket sat in the corner of Henry's room. It spilled over with the stories they had read throughout the years. Sometimes here; sometimes at the hospital. Claire knelt by the basket to pick out a story. She chose the one about trucks, knowing it was a favorite.

Standing, she noticed he was still wearing his cape. "You know I don't like you wearing your cape to bed."

"I know, Mommy, I forgot, but if I don't put it on after bath time, I leave it on the floor, and you don't like that either." Henry's bottom lip stuck out.

"It's okay Super Henry. You did good." Claire rumpled his damp hair.

Henry rolled over onto his side, tugging on the tail of the cape. With one good yank, he freed it and pulled it off over his head. He handed the prized possession to her. "Here, Mommy."

The cape was a gift to Henry from a group of nurses at the clinic where he receives his treatments. They told him his super power was smiling, and he needed a cape to go with it. It had a large SH on it – for

Super Henry. Now, it's what they all called him. Even she used the nickname. It gave her hope.

"Thank you." Claire took the cape and hung it on the bedpost. "Now, are you ready for the truck story?"

"Oh yes." Henry's eyes widened.

"You know," she said as she crawled up beside him and let him snuggle into her arms. "I interviewed with a construction company today, and they use lots of big trucks to build their houses."

"What kind?" Henry asked looking up into her face.

"Well, I suppose they have cement trucks to pour the foundations of the houses."

"Did you see one today?"

"No, honey, but I bet I will if I get the job."

"I'd like that job. I want to be a truck driver when I grow-up. I'll run over all the small cars in my way. Toot-toot!" Henry sat up and pumped his arm up and down, making his pretend horn blare. Claire recognized the motion as a good sign. Some days with Henry's condition, he couldn't lift his arms at all.

Claire propped the book up and made it dance towards Henry. "I'm coming, Super Henry, to read to you."

Henry squealed.

Claire gathered him back into her arms. "I love you."

"Awe, Mommy." He wiggled as she tried to kiss him. She let him go, soaking in his giggles.

"How about a hug?" She asked not sure what her five-year-old would do.

Henry threw his arms around her neck and squeezed tight. She soaked this in too.

After the story, Henry closed his eyes to pray. Claire sat on the edge of his bed watching. As a child, she had been taught to pray before bedtime, and she had passed that on to Henry – a tradition of sorts

"And please let Mommy get this job with the big trucks so I can drive them… someday." Henry looked up at his mom, jerked his head back down to his chest and added, "bless Baby. Amen."

"Where is Baby?" Claire asked, looking around for the ragged brown teddy bear.

"I think he fell down the crack again."

"Again? It eats anything that gets near it. Last week, it ate your sock and three plastic Indians."

"Can you look under the bed? Please, Mommy?" Henry snuggled under his covers and pulled them up to his nose.

"Okay, but you owe me one good-night kiss for this." Claire got down on all fours, then poked her head up. "If I'm not back in five minutes, you know the crack ate me."

"Mooooom."

"Okay, I'm only kidding." Claire smiled to herself. She knew she'd pay for the remark later tonight when Henry woke up swearing the crack was going to eat him. Oh well, you only live once.

Claire dug around under the bed. "Found him!" She popped up beside the bed and in a deep voice said, "Here I am."

"Baby." Henry grabbed the bear and hugged him.

"Hey, you owe me one kiss, super guy." Claire put her cheek next to Henry's face, and he gave her a quick peck. "Oh, my hero." She said, clasping her hands together and laying her freshly kissed cheek on them.

"Moooom!" He giggled.

Claire raised to her feet and walked to the door.

"Good-night, sleep tight." Claire turned off the light, then started to close the door.

"Can you leave it open?"

"Yes, half-way. Now, go to sleep."

"Good-night." Henry's voice sounded so small to her against the quiet and emptiness of the house.

In the kitchen, Claire poured herself a glass of tea and sat at the table where she had left the stacks of bills.

There were the regular ones: utilities, phone, rent, but it was the others that bothered her the most because they represented all the tears and pain she and Henry had experienced.

Now, Henry needed infusions. They were expensive and consumed hours and days. How was she going to manage? She'd miss more work which meant less money. The monthly insurance premiums took half her paychecks when she had one, but without it, they'd be snowed under for sure. No, she had to keep the health insurance.

She sipped her tea and fought to swallow her tears with it. Crying didn't help, and if Henry heard her, it would upset him.

Praying helps. There was that nudging again. Her faith in God at best was shaky. She had been praying for years: first for her marriage and now for Henry, and nothing changed. Lately, when she did toss up a prayer, it took the form of an SOS signal or a rescue flare in the night sky.

Adele, the owner of the Café, had encouraged her to come to the First Community Church, but the few times she had gone she felt like such a fraud. They all seemed so…happy, no worries or cares. Her life revolved around worry and struggle.

Besides, she wasn't sure about this faithful God she kept hearing about. Once she had believed but now, she didn't know. The man she thought would be with her forever had up and left in the moment of her greatest need. How could she trust a God she couldn't see to be there when the man she loved wouldn't even stay?

"Pray," she muttered and swatted the word away with the wave of her hand.

She turned her focus to the stack, sitting in front of her, willing herself to take the one on top and start.

∞

The trash bag, Haden dragged behind him, threatened to burst. He pushed in the Chinese take-out boxes and shoved in a two-liter bottle he found behind a stack of files on the counter close to his desk. The black plastic stretched.

"I see you've been motivated," said Kyle as he entered Haden's office.

"I took a deep breath yesterday and didn't like what I smelled. Is Jed here yet?"

"He sent a text. The Thomas project hit a few snags. He said he was running a little late, but he should be here any minute." Kyle took a seat in one of the two chairs, facing Haden's desk. "Wow, you had a computer under there?"

"Smart-alec. I'll have you know this is the third bag I've filled so far and not all of this trash is mine. We've let this place go."

"Hey, you're the one who kept hiring and firing. They weren't here long enough to get to the cleaning."

Haden turned, pinning his cousin Kyle with a look. Undeterred, Kyle continued, "You didn't happen to find a pocket knife, did you? I've been looking for my gray one with an eagle engraved on it, since June."

"Well, since it's April, I guess the jokes on you, but I'll keep my eye out for it."

"Thanks," said Kyle as the sound of the door closing bounced down the hallway.

"Hey," Jed entered the office with a cup of coffee in hand.

"Any for us?" Kyle asked.

"What? Do I look like a delivery service? Besides, it's from earlier this morning when I had to get up at O-dark thirty to be at the Thomas site."

"Well, don't leave the cup lying around here when you're done with it. Make sure it gets into the trash can."

"Do we have one of those?" Kyle asked; Jed laughed.

"Ha-Ha." Haden decided to abandon his trash pick-up in favor of getting the meeting started. Otherwise, his two knuckle headed partners would be around longer than he could handle.

He loved his brother and cousin; after all, they had grown up together, but at times, like now, their antics drove him crazy. At least here at the office, they kept it low key. At home on holidays, it got worse.

"Alright," said Haden as he plopped into his squishy leather chair.

"I want to talk about Claire Reed."

Jed took the empty seat next to Kyle.

"She's great, isn't she?" Jed grinned like a school boy with a crush.

"What do we know about her?" asked Kyle.

"From what Jed told me and from what I saw yesterday, she seems more than qualified."

"Great. She's hired. Now, I can get back to the Thomas job." Jed started to rise.

"Hold up a minute. That's not all there is."

Jed shrugged. "What else?"

"There's a hiccup. Her son has a medical condition. It's why she can't keep a job."

"Oh, so that's what she meant the other day at the café. About her son being the issue," said Jed.

Haden continued, "Yeah, they have a lot of doctor's appointments and what she calls maintenance."

"How will it affect her working situation?" Kyle leaned back in his chair and crossed his ankles.

"That's what I asked her. She said flexible hours would help. So, I told her I would run it by you guys and see if she could work forty hours anytime between six in the morning and six in the evening, Monday through Saturday. It would give her room to adjust her schedule when she needed the afternoon off for Henry."

"Hey, that's Grandpa's name," said Jed.

"That sounds like the solution." Kyle placed his hands on his knees and pushed himself up.

"I'm not sure. There'll have to be a lot of adjusting. We won't know what time of day she'll be here. It could be morning or late afternoon. I can't say yes with this much uncertainty."

Kyle sat back down

"Well, you must've liked her, or you wouldn't have tried to work something out." Jed flattened his lips into a straight line.

"I guess it was her openness. I mean she was honest about the whole thing. She could've kept quiet, and the job would've been hers. But there's something else."

Jed and Kyle sat, staring at Haden.

Kyle broke the silence. "Are you going to tell us or do we have to read your mind?"

Haden paused not wanting to air his own grievances against Claire, then said, "She's sassy."

"Yes, she is," said Jed. "Noticed that right off. It's what made me think she'd fit right in. I mean with us. You have to be sassy to survive the Sawyer Clan."

"I'm with Jed. She needs a little backbone to make it with us and all the men who are in and out of this place. If she were a wall flower, she'd wilt."

"Okay," said Jed. "Let's take a vote. I vote we hire her."

"Me too," said Kyle. They both looked at Haden, waiting for his vote. He scooted back in his chair and placed his hands across his middle – his thinking posture.

"I don't know, guys. Y'all didn't see the look she had on her face when she saw this mess."

"No, but I did see the look you had on your face when you shook her hand," said Jed. "You're afraid. She's a beautiful woman, and you're afraid."

"Sarah sure did a number on you," said Kyle.

Haden bolted up right in his chair. "I vote no."

"Doesn't matter. Kyle and I voted yes, so two against one. Besides, we have to hire someone before Mom goes in for her surgery."

"Jed's right. We need someone to help keep the doors open while Aunt Betty is in the hospital. You know my mom will be busy taking care of her. So, she can't help us here."

"Yeah, it's good for everyone. Claire needs a job, and we need Claire. You're going to have to put aside whatever is bothering you, for Mom's sake." Jed said.

"Fine." The knot in Haden's stomach tightened with his words. "But the two of you are helping me get this place in shape before I call her to let her know."

Haden agreed they needed someone; he only wished that someone didn't have nice curves and look so cute when she got mad.

Haden crushed the soda can before placing it in the trash bag. After all his hard work, keeping to himself, letting the hurt heal. How on earth was he supposed to ignore a woman like Claire Reed?

Chapter Five

The clang of the filing cabinet closing sounded like music to Haden's ears. Cymbals in a marching band maybe but still music.

Claire had started on Monday and had taken full control of the administrative duties with gusto. She filed, made entries into the computer, and chiseled the black goo off the front burner of the stove. The place hadn't looked this good since Lorraine.

Her ability to adapt had also impressed him. She didn't flinch when there were changes in the foremen's schedules as one construction job ended and another began. She juggled the necessary paperwork and contracts without complaint. He hated it, but he couldn't help comparing her to Sarah, who had complained when things didn't go according to plan.

Haden's mind ran back to the last month they had been together. Sarah, absorbed in the planning of the wedding, had pushed for everything to be perfect. Working, pressing, until it was all her way. She hadn't noticed Haden's reluctance. She'd missed the fact that he'd stopped planning.

Haden stood in the doorway of his office and took a deep breath to clear his mind. The air smelled sweet, clean. In it lingered the hint of lavender, Claire's scent. The fact he knew this only after a week made him uneasy.

He heard Claire chatting with Jed. It didn't escape his attention that Jed had hung around the office more than usual, using any excuse to see her. Another fact that made him uneasy.

It was time for him to move along. Haden left the work covering his desk and joined them in the receptionist area.

"Jed, shouldn't you be finishing up with the Thomas house? I mean it's Friday, and we do have a schedule. You know that thing we try to keep."

Jed, who was leaning against Claire's desk with his legs crossed at his ankles, didn't move. "I checked in before lunch, and everything is humming along. At this point, I'd be in the way."

Haden noted he said this more to Claire who was standing at the filing cabinets, than to him.

"You seem okay with being in the way," said Haden, kicking Jed's boots as he went by towards the kitchen. The force of the kick caused Jed's foot to hit the floor with a thud. He jumped up.

Claire tittered.

"Claire seems to think we're funny," commented Jed.

Diverting his gaze from the day-old sandwich in the refrigerator, Haden glanced her way. "Yeah, she asked during her interview if we fight much. I lied to her." Haden caught Claire's warm smile as it spread across her face and couldn't help but smile himself.

"You two remind me of my little boy." Her vibrant green eyes twinkled as she turned toward him. "always looking for mischief."

He held her gaze, thinking her eyes reminded him of the color of grass in the spring.

Afraid she knew what he was thinking, Haden turned back to the sandwich and half-finished cola, but his mind stayed on Claire and her green eyes and…

"Umm, you smell so sweet," said Jed. "What's that scent you're wearing?"

Haden slammed the refrigerator door shut. "I'm going to Adele's. Anyone want anything? And by anyone," He said, shooting Jed a dirty look. "I mean Claire."

"I already ate anyway." Jed resumed his original position.

"Claire, how 'bout you?"

"Oh, I would love a piece of her chocolate cake." Claire licked her lips. Haden made a hasty exit.

Good Lord, a woman who eats. Haden knew Jed was in trouble. Her eyes sparkled, she smelled good like a soft summer wind, and she ate. Jed might as well start looking for the wedding invitations. Haden shook his head as he trudged along the sidewalk, heading to Adele's café. Poor Jed.

∞

Adele assessed the situation. She knew her nephew well enough to know what a double bacon cheeseburger meant. It was his go to frustration fuel. She had served it to him each lunch before he fired the latest secretary.

"So, how's Claire doing?" She wiped the counter in front of Haden. She had been sure they would find their footing. She hoped she wasn't wrong.

"She's fine. The place hasn't run this smooth since Lorraine." Haden scowled.

He must've heard the rumors about Sarah. She hated to be the one to tell him, maybe this let her off the hook. "So, you heard."

"Heard what? You hear a lot of things in this town."

"You ordered a double bacon cheeseburger. It tends to mean

trouble is brewing. I thought you'd heard… about Sarah."

"Sarah? You mean leave two weeks before the wedding, Sarah?"

Apparently, he hadn't heard the rumors flying around town about her returning to work for one of the local architects.

Adele braced herself against the counter. "Yes, that Sarah."

"What've you heard?" Haden's voice hardened.

"Just that she might be returning, to work for one of the local architects. I think it's the Baldwin company."

"Well, this day just keeps getting better and better." Haden shook his head.

Cherie came up behind Adele and slid Haden's order in front of him. Without hesitation, he took a hunk out of the burger.

"What else has happened?" Adele asked.

"I can't seem to get Jed out of the office since Claire started. He finds every excuse to hang around. What am I going to do? It's been a week, and I'm thinking about changing the locks to keep him out."

"You didn't seem to mind him hanging around when the second one was there, what was her name."

"Michelle or Margaret, something with an M. He wasn't in the way as much I guess. But now he's everywhere. Every time I turn around, I'm bumping into him. The office isn't big enough for both of us." Haden chomped down another bite and started in on the fries.

"Umm, I see." Adele didn't buy Haden's explanation. "Is Claire complaining about him hanging around?"

The sharp V of his brows returned. "No. She isn't." Haden stuffed a fistful of fries into his mouth.

Once he swallowed, he asked, "What else do you know about Sarah?"

"I heard she's supposed to be here in a couple of weeks. I wanted to tell you so you'd have time to prepare. I didn't want you running into her on the street and be caught off guard."

"Yeah, that'd be fun. 'Hi Sarah, how have you been? Oh, and thanks for leaving me to tell everyone the wedding was off.'" Haden let out a groan and tore another piece from the burger. "I guess it's what I deserved." He mumbled around the food as he dipped his fries in ketchup.

Adele reached across the counter and patted his hand. "You may find your heart has healed more than you think. The Lord has a way of keeping us from making mistakes, even if it hurts at the time."

"I know you're right. It would've been a mistake for me to have married Sarah. We wanted different things.

"To be honest, I've been toying with the idea of dating again. But when it comes to Sarah, my heart and pride took a beating. I'm not sure I can do the good neighbor thing with her even if I'm ready to move on." Haden leaned back into the chair.

"You're under construction, Haden. We all are. The Lord has a plan watch and see. You'll be able to face her when the time comes."

Haden shook his head. "It's a little more complicated than that."

∞

The papers scattered all over Haden's desk attested to his attempt to keep busy. His mind kept wandering back to his conversation with his Aunt Adele. It popped up unbidden. Sarah was moving back to Miller Creek. What was he going to do now? She'd left, and he hadn't explained to anyone why.

Haden's cell phone buzzed, pulling him from his thoughts. "What now?" he groused. A picture of his mother smiled back at him from the display.

"Hey Mom, what's up?" He leaned back, getting comfortable in his chair.

"I hate to bother you at work, but I wanted to remind you about Tuesday's appointment with the anesthesiologist. I know you and Jed said you wanted to be there…so,"

"Yes, we did. You were right to call and remind me. I've been a little distracted. I'll have to let my secretary know I'll be out that morning."

"Your Aunt Adele told me you hired a new administrative assistant. How's she working out?"

"Fine. She's great." He wanted to tell her all about Jed's mooning over Claire but thought better of it. His mom tended to play matchmaker throwing in with his Aunt Adele. The two of them were always going on about this sweet young woman or that pretty dear thing. They both swore they wanted what was best for the them, but Haden surmised it was a plot for getting grandchildren.

"She also told me about Sarah. How are you handling it?"

"I don't have to handle it, Mom." A pang of guilt hit Haden the moment the words left his lips.

"Sorry, sweetie, I didn't mean to bring up old issues."

"I'm the one who's sorry. I didn't mean to snap at you. I guess I better get used to people asking me about her. It's inevitable they will."

"Her calling off the wedding two weeks before, left people with questions." Haden hadn't bothered to correct his mother over the details. Now, he wondered if he should. "So, have you given it any thought? About what you might do with her in town?"

"There's not much I can do. She's moving back; I'm not moving away. So, that leaves me with being civil when I have to see her and avoiding her like the plague when I can."

"In this town? Miller Creek isn't that big."

"Well, that's what I'm going to do."

"At least you've had a year to get over her. You are over her, right?"

Haden paused before answering. His heart had been broken, but it mended. He knew her leaving had been a blessing in disguise. "I am. It's my pride that still stings a little."

"That's what I figured, but it'll heal too. Will you be at the house Sunday?"

"I don't think so."

"Okay, see y'all on Tuesday then. Don't forget to remind Jed when you see him. I couldn't get a hold of him."

"Yeah, he's been a little preoccupied as well. I'll be sure to tell him when I see him." Which he knew would be any minute, the way he'd been acting.

Haden sighed as the feeling of dread washed over him. He knew his mom was right; avoidance wouldn't work. What he needed was something to deter the questions which were bound to crop up and maybe keep Sarah at a distance at the same time. Something to prove he was over her.

Chapter Six

Late Friday afternoon, Claire sat at her desk working, absorbed in the music coming from the radio. Her favorite station played a collection of 40's, 50's and 60's songs, and she had the volume up full blast. She found the music helped her to focus.

Whether she wanted to admit it or not, her new boss distracted her. The first few days, Jed's interruptions helped to keep her thoughts off of Haden. But that tactic hadn't worked for long. The music seemed to do the trick.

Claire hummed along with the song Chances Are as she typed, focused on the information she needed to add to their standard contract.

Haden's face popped up above her computer screen, and she screeched, jumping back with her hand over her heart.

"You scared me," She reached over and turned off the radio. Her heart racing.

"Sorry, I needed to let you know Jed and I will be out of the office Tuesday. We have a family matter to attend to."

"Tuesday? Umm…" Claire stood, looking down at her desk calendar. "I was going to talk to you before I left this evening. I need Tuesday off. Henry has an infusion."

"Can you reschedule?"

"I don't know if I can at this point." Claire hated it to be inconvenient the first time she needed off. That's how it started.

Haden crossed his arms over his broad chest which narrowed to a tight waist. His shirt outlined his physic.

"I'll ask Kyle to come into the office." Haden shifted his stance.

Claire caught herself staring and looked away.

Uncomfortable, she looked back down at her desk calendar. "Oh, that would be great. I'll try to give you more notice in the future when I need the whole day off." She grabbed a pen and made a note on Tuesday's square.

Haden held up his hands. "That's alright. It was part of the agreement, you having flexible hours to take care of Henry."

"Do you think Kyle will mind?"

"No, but you might. He's a worse slob than me. No telling what condition the office will be in once he's done."

"It's one day. How much damage could he do?"

Haden's dimples popped out as his grin broadened. "You'd be surprised. There was one time when Lorraine was out with sinus problems, and I had been out of the office several days straight working at a site." Haden leaned his hip against the desk, moving him closer to her.

Claire could smell the outdoors mingled with a musky scent on him. "When she got back, she couldn't find her desk for all the mess he had piled on it, cartons, drink cans. If you thought the place was a sty when you started, you should have seen it that week. Lorraine said she found some chicken feathers strowed throughout the trailer."

"Oh, dear, what from?"

"I don't know. Neither one of us was brave enough to ask him, and Kyle works on a 'don't ask, don't tell' policy. If you don't ask, he doesn't tell." Claire found herself smiling at Haden's story, wrapped up in the warmth of family it radiated.

∞

Claire remembered to bring the iPad with Henry's favorite movies down-loaded on it. She used it as a special treat for him, every time they came to the hospital for an infusion. He would be well entertained over the next eight hours as they administered the immunoglobulin into the child's blood stream.

Claire sat in the wide blue chair that resembled an oversized lazy boy recliner. Henry climbed up into her lap. He settled himself, pulling the tail of his cape out from under him. She sat his backpack in the chair beside them.

She winced when the needle went into her son's small arm. Henry didn't make a sound. She wrapped the tail of his cape around him as he sat in her lap. It never ceased to amaze her how gentle the nurses were with him.

"Henry is one of our favorite patients," said Jennifer, the younger of the two nurses as she taped the IV into place.

"Yes, he is. He's our Super Henry," agreed Pat as she checked his vital signs.

They got Henry a second overbed table and placed it in front of the chair. Claire fiddled with the iPad case and got it set up for him. He couldn't hold it. His arms had grown weaker over the last week. His muscles did that right before time for a treatment.

After an hour of animated trains, Claire's stomach began to growl.

She caught the other nurse as she passed by them. "Do you mind if

I step down to the cafeteria? I didn't eat before we came."

"Go ahead. We'll keep Henry company while you're gone." Pat smiled and winked at her.

"Where are you going, Mommy?" asked Henry as she slid him off her lap. The blue chair swallowed him.

"Just down the hall for a few minutes. The nurses will be here, though, and I'll be back in a flash." Claire grabbed her wallet, setting her purse on the side table where Henry could see it. He knew she never went far without it.

Before leaving, she dug around in the backpack for Baby. Setting the worn brown bear next to Henry, she leaned over, and placed a kiss on his forehead. "See ya in a minute."

Henry drew the bear to his side and waved to her with his free hand. His gaze glued to the screen of his iPad

As Claire neared the waiting room of the anesthesiology department, she heard familiar voices. She had to pass down this hall to get to the cafeteria, but she didn't want Jed or Haden to think she was intruding on them.

She'd slip by and wouldn't stop, but she couldn't help looking through the observation glass which separated the hall and the waiting room, to get a glimpse of their mother.

Haden's eyes met hers; she looked away. Haden appeared in the doorway. "Hi Claire." His voice boomed, the sheer volume enough for the gray-haired woman at the end of the hall to shoot them a look.

Jed turned her direction and acknowledged Claire with a nod.

"Hi, yourself. Are you alright?"

"Fine, honey." He said as he smiled at his family. Haden grabbed her shoulders and pushed her back a step or two away from the entrance of the waiting room. Now, Claire knew something was up.

"Honey?"

As Claire's brows crinkled, Haden leaned forward like he was going to kiss her cheek, but instead, whispered, "Follow my lead."

He let go of her shoulders and captured her hand. Before she could answer, Haden dragged her into the waiting room and deposited her in front of an older woman whom she assumed was his mother.

"So, this is Claire. I've heard so much about you from Adele. It's great to put a face to the name."

"Yes, Adele is wonderful. She's the one who helped me get my job with Haden and Jed." Claire nodded.

"That's what she tells me, but she didn't say a word about you and Haden dating."

Claire stood with her mouth gapping open like a big mouth bass. "Aaahh? Yeah…" She looked to Haden for an explanation.

"I think Claire's a little surprised herself…that Aunt Adele didn't tell you," Jed said with a twinkle in his eyes.

Haden cut in. "Honey, I thought it would be best to let the family in on our little secret. I know we agreed not to say anything since you were going to be working with me, but we live in the twenty first century. So, the cats out of the bag, so to speak."

"That's some cat. Does it have rabies?" Claire didn't like where this was going.

"Isn't she cute?" said the woman sitting next to Betty. "I can see

Haden will have his hands full with you." She said this with a warm smile on her face, but the tone left Claire with a chill. This got under her skin, and she gave Haden's hand a firm squeeze to pass along her displeasure. Haden dropped her hand and flexed his.

"Claire, this is Sarah Dempsey." Haden's eyes filled with pleading as he made these introductions.

"Nice to meet you." Claire held out her hand to the slim, well dressed woman. She didn't take it. Instead, she reached down and picked up the briefcase, sitting at her feet. Claire retracted her stranded hand.

"Yes, it's nice to meet you as well." She stood and addressed Betty. "I had wanted to stop by and check on you since I was here this morning, meeting with the board about the remodeling."

"I'm so glad you did, Sarah."

"Well, we were almost family." Here, she paused. If looks could kill, Claire knew she'd be dead. "And you've always been so good to me." Sarah leaned down and hugged Betty. "I'll be sure to come by and see you after your surgery."

"Oh, that would be great."

Turning to Jed, she said, "A pleasure, as always."

Jed saluted her with his right hand, while holding a coffee cup in his left.

Then facing Haden, she stepped forward and planted a kiss on each cheek as if she lived in France. Claire's lips thinned into a tight line.

"It's so good to see you, Haden." She reached out and clasped his hand in hers "I've missed our friendship. But I'm sure we'll be bumping into one another a little more often, now that I'm back in town."

Claire fought the urge to slap her hand away, but before she could act, Sarah released him and sashayed towards the door.

Unable to keep quiet, she called out "wonderful meeting you. I'm sure I'll be bumping into you as well."

Sarah stopped and turned. Claire didn't flinch.

"I'll be looking forward to it," said Sarah.

Claire met her icy gaze. "Me, too." Then she reached out and took Haden's hand.

Sarah shrugged and marched to the door.

Claire turned her attention back to the three people still staring at her.

"Do you think she bought it?" asked Claire, looking at Haden.

Haden gave her hand a little squeeze. "Bought what, darling?"

Claire confused, started to get irritated. Sarah was gone. There was no need to keep up this pretense.

Jed, who had been quiet during the exchange, working on his coffee, said, "I think she bought the whole farm."

"Don't be silly. Sarah hasn't been in town long enough to buy any property. Besides, what would she do with a farm?" Betty tsked.

"You're right, Mom. I don't know what I was thinking."

With a scowl lingering on her face, Betty asked, "So, Claire tell me a little about yourself."

"Well, I'm a mom." With those words, Betty Sawyer's face lit up like fireworks on the fourth of July.

"Oh, how perfect."

∞

Haden and Claire sat in the back corner of the hospital cafeteria. Somehow, Haden managed to break free from his mom in order to explain things to Claire. Jed had agreed to drive Betty home.

"Look, I know I shouldn't have told my mom we're dating, but…"

"No, but's. You need to get this straightened out. I don't want her having any false hopes. Did you see the way her eyes lit up when I talked about Henry? She's already baking cookies and playing go fish."

"I know," said Haden. "She's been after me and Jed to settle down for years because she wants grand kids. She thinks since I'm nearing thirty it might never happen."

"I understand but telling her we're dating is not going to help. She'll just be disappointed when the truth comes out."

"I can't tell her the truth."

"Sure, you can. You string these words together 'I'm not dating Claire.' Easy." Claire bit into her whole-wheat toast.

"No, I can't. If she thinks I'm single, she'll be working double time to get me back together with Sarah. She never did see the big picture where Sarah was concerned." And Haden knew he hadn't drawn it out too clearly for her either.

"So, what is the big picture? I mean, since I'm your girlfriend and all, I ought to know." Claire's vivid green eyes sparkled. Haden saw the warmth they held.

He cleared his throat. "Sarah came into my life right after my Dad passed away. She was compassionate, caring. Everything I needed at the time."

"It sounds like she cared for you a great deal." Claire's features softened.

"She did, and we dated for about a year." Haden picked up a napkin and twisted it. "Let's just say things didn't work out like I had hoped they would."

"That doesn't tell me much." Claire pushed her half-eaten food aside.

"The problems showed up when we started talking about the future. Our ideas of what life should look like were miles apart. What she wanted and what I wanted didn't match up."

"What happened?"

"I thought we could work it out. She said she was willing to be open minded." Haden stopped not sure how much to tell her. "But as you know, she left."

"She left?" Claire reached out and took hold of Haden's hand that still clutched the mutilated napkin. "I'm so sorry."

Haden lifted his eyes to meet hers. "Today was the first time I've seen her."

He leaned back in the chair, pulling his hand from hers. "When Mom started cooing about how good it was to see her, and asking me didn't she look great, I knew she wouldn't let it go. She and Aunt Adele have been playing matchmaker for years. I panicked."

"So, you tossed me under the bus."

Chapter Seven

Claire, although flattered he thought of her as girlfriend material, knew she was handy. The man had no social life as far as she could tell. He was all business, all the time.

Haden cringed. "I guess I did drag you into the middle of it. I just couldn't stand the thought of disappointing Mom, with her sick and all, but Sarah is not an option, and you were the first person I thought of…Sorry."

A cafeteria worker passed by their table as he moved through the back area picking up abandoned plates and cups.

"Are you sure it's over? Cause she's still carrying a torch for you."

"She could be carrying a volcanic eruption for me; it doesn't make a difference. It's taken a year and a mound of bacon cheeseburgers to get over her, but it's done. My main concern is my mom. This cancer talk scars me."

"I'm sure she'll be fine." Claire stifled a groan. She hated spouting platitudes.

Haden got a distant look in his eyes. "She sits down when no one is looking. She wants us all to think everything's the same, but I know better." His gaze fell on her. "I know she's being strong for Jed and me."

Claire couldn't stand it. She rose from her seat, wrapped her arms around Haden, half assaulting him, and squeezed all the compassion she had for him out of her heart into his.

It took a moment, but Haden's arms slid around Claire drawing her into his lap. She let him, wanting to comfort him.

He nestled his head into the crook of her neck. Claire whispered, "Oh Haden, I know this must be hard." The scent of him made her head light. She closed her eyes.

She raised her head to kiss his forehead, but before she did, someone dropped a tray. Her eyes popped open, and she pushed herself ram rod straight.

"I'm sooo sorry." Claire said as she tried to extract herself from Haden's lap.

Haden, too, seemed to become aware of their surroundings and popped out of his chair like it was on fire. Claire grabbed the table to keep from hitting the floor.

"I don't know what to say." Haden's wide eyes told Claire all she needed to know. "This was a mistake. I mean…I don't usually do this sort of thing. I mean I barely know you. I mean…"

"I know what you mean!" Claire couldn't believe she had put herself in this position. What had come over her? He was her boss.

"Claire, I."

Claire snatched her wallet from the table.

"You, Haden Sawyer, need to get this matter with your mother straightened out. We need to keep our relationship professional. I don't have time for this; I've got Henry I need to worry about." Claire gasped and looked at her watch.

"Oh no." She grabbed her cafeteria tray and dashed for the trash can.

Haden followed. "Look, Claire, I'm sorry about what happened, but

I can't tell my mom we're not dating. It's not only Sarah, okay. You saw how her eyes lit up when she heard about Henry. That's the liveliest I've seen her in months. If I tell her we aren't dating, she'll be so disappointed. Let me give her some joy, something to look forward to."

Claire dumped the tray and whipped around. "Look, I need to get back to Henry. I can't talk about this, right now. I know the truth is always the best way."

"We will tell her the truth, just not yet."

"WE…" A groan escaped Claire's lips as she propped one hand on her hip and pointed at Haden with the other one. "No, you tell her today before it goes too far."

∞

Haden stood, looking at himself in the bathroom mirror as he shaved.

He cringed. The blade of his razor left a gash in his chin. He dropped the razor and snatched at the toilet paper roll hanging on the wall. The dispenser whirled as the paper spun out of control.

The bags under his eyes attested to his restless night's sleep. Crankiness hung all over him. The blood on his chin highlighted the point.

Dabbing at the cut, Haden muttered. "Why should I tell Mom we're not dating? It'll only create trouble. She'll be 'why don't you ask Sarah out' and 'she's such a nice girl'. Nice girl my eye."

Haden tossed the blood-stained paper into the trash and wrestled his brown curls into submission. "Do nice girls leave their ex-fiancés to clean up the mess? Nooo. To explain to every stinking Tom, Dick, and Adele why?" Staring into the mirror, he confessed, "I guess I deserved it though."

As he backed up to examine the cut in the mirror, he banged his head on the door frame. His hand shot to his head. Pain spread across his skull, and he stomped his foot. Sarah wasn't the problem, and he knew it.

Claire.

She had issued the truth mandate, and he'd ignored it. He didn't like deceiving anyone, ever, but now, he had lied to his mom and dragged Claire into his problems. Then there was the whole issue of what had really happened with Sarah.

"First things first, what am I going to tell Claire?" He asked himself as he rubbed the knot that laid beneath his hair.

"Are you talking to yourself again?"

Haden jumped. "I ought to lay you out right here for taking ten years off my life."

Jed chuckled. "You know talking to yourself is a sure sign of spending too much time alone, right."

"What are you doing traipsing through my house anyway?"

"Well, when you didn't answer the doorbell, I thought I ought to check on you. Now, I see you were engrossed in an in-depth conversation with your alter ego. Did you guys come to any decisions?"

"What are you talking about?" Haden reached passed Jed to retrieve his shirt from the hook on the back of the door.

"About what you're going to tell Claire. I thought it was a real bold move on your part to claim her as your girlfriend."

"Is that what this visit is about? Not worried I'm dead in here after all?"

"Oh no, I was concerned, but since you guys brought it up…" Jed motioned towards the mirror with his thumb.

Haden glared at Jed as he skirted passed him and headed down the hall to the kitchen.

Sarah and Haden had picked out the house. It was a small two-bedroom bungalow on one of the older streets in Miller Creek. It sat a few blocks from Main Street which made it convenient to Sawyer Construction and Aunt Adele's café.

After Sarah had left, he decided to keep it. He told himself he had liked the house well enough, and he needed a place to live since he'd given up his apartment. But if truth be told, he wanted to prove to everyone her leaving hadn't bothered him. Now, the house had become his. It no longer reminded him of Sarah.

"So, what are you going to do? Did you get a chance to talk to Claire yesterday after Mom and I left?"

"Boy, you're one big question mark today, aren't you?" Haden took two coffee mugs out of the cabinet. He filled one and handed it to Jed. The other, he put two teaspoons of sugar in before filling it.

"I'm not sure what I'm going to tell her."

"Well, you guys talked, right?" Haden sensed Jed's urgency.

"Yeah, we talked, but she wanted me to come clean with Mom, and I know if I do Mom will start after me about Sarah."

"Maybe not. After all, she's the one who called it off, right?" Jed sipped his coffee as he leaned his hip against the counter.

Haden cut his eyes toward Jed unwilling to answer the question. "You know once Mom and Aunt Adele get into their matchmaker mode there's no safe place. Besides, did you see how Mom lit up when she heard Claire talk about Henry."

"Boy, did I. You sure messed up with that. I'd hate to be in your shoes."

"I know; I know."

"You made it ten times harder to tell her you lied."

"I know; I know."

"If you had kept it to a fake girlfriend, you might have gotten off easy, but you added the potential of a grandson. After the last couple of years, you should know better. Grandmother hood is Aunt Adele's and Mom's final destination on this cruise of life."

"I know!" Haden slumped over the counter placing his elbows on the surface. "She's going to kill me."

"Which one?" asked Jed as he tossed the last few drops of his coffee into the sink. "Mom or Claire?"

"More than likely, both."

∞

Once Jed left for the Henderson site, Haden decided to grab his jacket and walk to the office. The sun was shining, and the trees moved in the light April breeze. He needed the time to think before he came face-to-face with Claire.

Claire swept into his thoughts as natural as the wind swept around him. She was warm and smelled sweet like the morning air. Haden smiled, thinking of the hospital. Her arms wrapped around him as he nuzzled in her hair.

Heat rose on the back of his neck as he remembered the scent of her hair and the softness of her touch. The lightness of her body against him.

Haden reached up and ran his hand through his hair. She was his employee. He had to get a handle on his thoughts.

His boots thudded against the sidewalk as he lengthened his stride. Then, there was Jed. He'd called it right. He'd lied, but he knew if he told his mom Claire wasn't his girlfriend, she'd launch an all-out campaign to get Sarah back into his life. Haden envisioned Sunday dinners at his moms with Sarah present or bumping into her due to his mom's efforts.

But a lie was a lie.

Haden was uncomfortable with that word. He didn't think of himself as a Godly man, but he'd been raised in the church and lying was a no-no. Here he was though, up to his eyeballs in them.

As he rounded the corner onto Main street, he caught sight of Claire and a little boy, he assumed was Henry, entering Adele's Café.

He stopped. The morning sun caught her features as she looked down talking to the child. For a split second, the effect illuminated her face. One word popped into his head.

Angel.

His heart raced. His thoughts scattered.

Frustrated with his reaction to her, Haden squared his shoulders, lifted his scabbed chin, and barreled forth, not even glimpsing in the direction of the Café.

Entering the trailer which housed his office, Haden muttered. "Angel." Shaking his head, he added, "I've got to get a grip."

"I don't know about angels, but I'm gonna be a dead man once

Claire gets a look at this place."

Haden let out a low whistle as he surveyed the damage. He spotted Kyle sitting at Claire's desk, half- hidden by the stacks of files. "How did you do this in twenty-four hours? Did you stay up all night to make sure the place was a wreck?"

"It's a talent." Kyle stood.

Haden scowled. "Man, we better get busy. I saw Claire and her son go into your mom's café. We don't have long."

"Where do we start?"

Haden let out a sigh. "I ought to leave you to Claire."

"I know, but why do you think I'm here and not out on site. I was trying to get the place back into some semblance of order before either one of you got here. Besides, you need me. Who else can do the specialty wood working we offer?"

"That and that alone is saving your hide. Go get a trash bag and pick up your…litter. I'll see if I can't get most of these files back into the right drawers."

Kyle walked across the small space to the kitchen and dug a black plastic trash bag out from under the sink.

Haden took off his jacket and started sorting the files piled on Claire's desk. "Why are all these files out anyway? What were you doing with the files from ten years ago?"

"I thought I'd go through and do some purging. You know get rid of the ones we didn't need anymore, update everything."

Haden's groan sounded more like a growl. "Have you lost your mind? What on earth do you know about keeping anything up to date?"

"No need to get nasty."

"So, did you do any 'purging'?" Haden drew the word out.

"Well," Kyle stopped dropping soda cans into the bag and straightened. "I started, but…" Kyle's eyebrows rose high, and he cocked his head to the side, half shrugging.

Haden knew what was coming "What happened Kyle?"

"Daisey."

"I should have known it was a girl." Haden frowned as he began alphabetizing the first stack.

"Daisy's not just any girl. She could be the girl. If you'd been at Mom's the last few Sundays, you would've met her." Kyle went back to picking up the soda cans and empty chip bags.

"The girl. I don't think there is such a thing, one person for each of us. Think about how outnumbered men are to women in the population. What about all those women?" Haden jammed the first half of the alphabet back into the drawer labeled A- M.

"Sarah ruined you."

Haden grabbed the next stack. "Sarah, Sarah, Sarah. It's all I've heard since Aunt Adele told me she was coming back to town. I'm sick of it." Haden slammed his fist on the desk, making the pile jump. "It's bad enough I have to deal with her being here, but she showed up yesterday at the hospital." Haden dropped into the chair behind him.

A twinkle appeared in Kyle's eyes. "Well, if you're sick of talking about Sarah, why don't you tell me a little about Angel."

"Oh, for Pete's sake!"

Chapter Eight

Inside Adele's Café, Claire and Henry slid into one of the booths next to the window. She could see the yard of Sawyer Construction from her vantage point. Henry sat across from her his face covered by the menu.

"Good Morning, Henry, what can I get you?" Adele smothered a giggle.

"I think I'll start with coffee," answered Claire. "What do you want to drink?"

"Juice, please." Henry, emerged from behind the menu. He lifted it above his head with both hands and wore it like a hat.

"One coffee, one orange juice. I'll be right back." Adele took off without waiting for any further instructions.

The bell on the door jingled. "Welcome to Adele's Café," she sang out as two men entered and took seats at the counter.

"What do you want to eat?" Claire asked Henry, watching to make sure the menu didn't end up on the floor.

"What do they have?"

"Here are your choices." They went through this same ritual every time they ate at the Café. "They have eggs with bacon, or waffles, or chocolate chip pancakes." She saved the best till last, knowing Henry would order his favorite pancakes. It's what he got every time.

Claire needed this routine, something solid, normal. She had spent a restless night creating scenarios about seeing Haden. Her sheets looked as twisted up as her insides. Every time she dozed off, her dreams would lead her to places she didn't want to go.

She spent the night oscillated between anger and apprehension, indulging in all the what ifs. What if she falls for him, what if he doesn't like Henry, what if - he leaves?

Here her fears would take flight, and she would remember the hurt after Henry's father, Ryan, left.

"Mom, can we go see the big trucks?"

"What big trucks?" Claire dragged her thoughts back to Henry.

"The ones at your new job. The ones we prayed about."

"Not today. Mrs. Nolen is expecting you."

"Aww… Mom, I don't want to go to Mrs. Nolen's. Can't you stay home with me today?"

"I wish I could, but I took off yesterday. So, if we want me to pay for these chocolate chip pancakes, I need to go to work." Henry slouched in his seat.

"Will David be there?" He asked.

"Yes, he will."

Adele trotted back to their booth and deposited one juice and a mug of coffee on the table. Looking over her shoulder, she asked "Are you two ready to order?"

Claire looked around Adele to see what had caught her interest. There at the end of the counter sat Sarah with an empty plate in front of her.

"Claire, I am so happy to hear about you and Haden dating. The timing is perfect."

Claire choked on her coffee. She reached for the napkin dumping the silverware on the table.

"Dating?" She dabbed her chin.

"Yes, Betty told me. She is so excited, and you should hear how she goes on and on about our little Henry here." Adele beamed, winking at Henry who hid behind the menu.

"Oh Adele," Claire slumped back against the seat. "Haden may have exaggerated our relationship a bit."

"What do you mean? How can you exaggerate dating? Either you are or you aren't." Adele's fist rested on her hip.

Claire couldn't keep herself from looking over at Sarah.

Adele turned her head and nodded. "Oh, I see. Was Sarah present when Haden made his big announcement?"

"Yes." Claire sat forward and wrapped her hands around the coffee mug. The warmth made the cold inside of her feel better.

Why did she feel like a traitor? Haden shouldn't have told his mother they were dating.

Adele stood for a moment with her lips pursed. She looked over her shoulder at Sarah and back at Claire. "Claire, I'm going to give you a piece of advice, and I want you to hear me out."

"I'd appreciate any help you can give me." Claire knew Adele to be a wise woman when it came to people and relationships.

"I want you for the time being to go with the flow."

"Excuse me? Go with the flow." Claire couldn't believe her ears. "Don't you think being honest would be best?"

Claire looked over at Henry who leaned his head on the table, listening. "That's what my teacher says, 'honesty is the best police.'"

"You mean policy," corrected Claire.

"Well, it means to be truthful. Teacher says we shouldn't tell fibs." Henry looked over at Claire without lifting his head. "Can I have chocolate chip pancakes, now? Pleeesee."

Adele took out her pad and wrote down Henry's order.

"Henry, wait. Miss Adele and I are talking." Claire turned her attention back to Adele.

"I know, but I'm hungry."

"What do you mean go with the flow?"

"Look it won't do any good for anyone to come clean right now. With Betty's surgery coming up, this gives her something to look forward to. It gives her hope."

"Yeah, false hope." A lump formed in Claire's throat, making it hard to swallow.

"Regardless, it's still hope, and every bit helps. I also think it will help Haden adjust to Sarah being around again." Both Claire and Adele looked towards the counter where the well-dressed woman sat digging in her purse.

"He's convinced his mother will try to get them back together." Claire shifted her gaze back to Adele.

"I don't think he's wrong. Betty's pretty set on seeing her sons married and settled. This business with breast cancer has served to intensified it. That's why I think it'd be better if you wait until after her surgery…when she's in the clear and the threat is gone. Besides, she'll be less likely to try any matchmaking while she's having her chemo treatments."

"I don't know. I don't think it's good to get her hopes up for a grandchild. I mean I come with one built in. No waiting."

"I'm waiting, Mommy." Henry said while giving Adele a fierce scowl.

"Yes, you are sweetie."

"What do you say? Can I count on you to give us a little time?" Claire knew Adele was close to her sister-in-law. How could she refuse her?

"When is her surgery?"

"In about two weeks if everything goes according to plan. After that, we go with Henry's plan, honesty is the best policy."

"I'll think about it, but I'm still not comfortable," Claire watched Henry as she spelled the word. "F-i-b-b-i-n-g. It's not a good example. My gut says this isn't going to end well."

"You don't know that," said Adele with a smile on her face. "Besides, you can negotiate a raise out of the situation or at the very least, a few free dinners. If Haden elected you to be his girlfriend, you should demand the girlfriend treatment: dinners, movies, paid babysitters. Shoot for the works."

"Great. Now, I'm an extortionist."

"No honey, you're a woman looking to be treated like a lady."

Henry fidgeting in his booster seat started to chant "pancakes, pancakes, pancakes," as he waved the menu around like a protest poster.

"Make that a double. Today calls for chocolate."

"Coming right up." As she turned to leave, she stopped and asked, "what did Haden have to say about this? Did he have an opinion?"

"I don't know. I haven't seen him, yet, and when we talked yesterday, I don't think it helped to resolve any thing." With these words, Claire's mind conjured up a picture of Haden holding her and the feel of his arms firm and strong around her.

∞

Haden had been deep in a daydream about a field, a picnic, and a woman who smelled of lavender when he heard the trailer door close with a bang. Claire.

His cheeks flushed at being interrupted by the object of his musings.

He pushed himself from his chair to go see her. He didn't really want to go face the firing squad, but he didn't want to prolong the agony either. He needed to let her know he wasn't going to tell his mom. His conversation with Jed had convinced him this was not the time.

He'd come clean after the surgery, but until then, they'd have to work something out. He couldn't disappoint his mom. He had gone too far with the potential of a grandchild. Now, they were stuck for the next two weeks or so.

Claire sat at her desk, leaning over picking something up off the floor. Haden hoped he and Kyle had found all the trash. They had finished the clean-up in record time, and Kyle left while he could.

"What did you find?" asked Haden.

Claire jumped, bumping her head on the underside of her desk. "Shoot!"

"Sorry." Haden stopped in front of her desk. "You, all right?'

"I'm fine." She turned her back to him and started sorting through the mail.

"You should've seen this place before you got here. Kyle lived up to his reputation." Haden waited for a response. Claire rolled her chair to the wastebasket and deposited the junk mail.

The tension between them pushed Haden on to discuss the issue. No delays he'd promised himself. "Look Claire, we need to talk about…this."

"Do we? Can't you do the right thing and let's be done with it?"

His muscles tensed as he stood straighter. "It's not that simple."

Claire turned to face him. "Well, if I recall, it was that simple yesterday when you were telling your mom a big, fat whopper of a lie." Claire stood with her hands on her hips.

Haden crossed his arms and planted his feet. "What's done is done. There's no going back. I can't un-lie."

"Yes, you can. It's called telling the truth." Her eyes became small slits as she crossed her arms.

"I've made up my mind. I can't and won't tell my mother until after the surgery. She's got so much ahead of her with the chemo and radiation. What's one white lie if it gives her a little happiness right now while she can enjoy it."

"One white lie? You mean one white lie that's turning my world upside down. One white lie that puts me in a position where I'm having to lie to people I respect. I don't like it."

His resolve faltered when he saw the fury in her eyes. He hated being the reason for her anger.

"I guess I should be grateful you're not expecting me to do this until she's through the whole thing." Claire relaxed her stance. "But I don't relish the thought of hurting her when she's at such a vulnerable place."

He dropped his arms and leaned across the desk. "Look, I'm sorry. I know I shouldn't have lied. I know it's inconvenient for you."

"But you're not sorry enough to do anything about it."

"I'm desperate," he said as he stood. "Because of her diagnosis, she's been relentless with the talk of marriage and family. And now Sarah is here reminding her of what she's missing. I just need some time to figure out how to make this work."

Claire shook her head. "Adele said the same thing. She thinks we need to wait, too."

"Aunt Adele knows about this?" All the fire of the argument left him. "How does she know about it?"

"Your mom. She called and told her all about us dating and how excited she was. Oh, and let's not forget about how she went on and on about Henry." Claire groaned. "It seems we are the talk of the town, or we will be by the close of business today."

"Oh boy." Haden needed to sit down. He propped himself against the edge of Claire's desk. What had he thought would happen? His mother would keep it to herself?

Claire walked around the desk to sit beside him. She sat close enough he could smell the lavender scent she wore. "Okay, let's say I play along for a couple of weeks, getting your mom through surgery and a little time to recover. How is this going to work?"

"What do you mean?"

"Well, what's our plan? Are we going to go out for real, or do we pretend and make more stuff up? And what is our exit plan?"

"Exit plan? What are you talking about?"

"I mean how do we break up?"

"Wow, this is a first even for me, discussing the break up before the first date," said Haden.

Claire grinned, drawing his attention to her strawberry lips. "Yeah, it's a first for me too. I usually make it through at least one date, but that was before Ryan."

Haden shifted his gaze from her lips to her eyes. "Ryan's Henry's dad?"

"Yeah." Claire nodded, looking down at her tennis shoes. Regret flashed across her face. She possessed a beauty which came from her openness. It washed over her, making Haden want to reach out and caress her cheek. He clutched the edge of the desk instead. "I haven't dated since he left. You know not a lot of time; that sort of thing."

When Claire met his gaze, with her eyes soft and searching, he felt compelled to say, "Well, we'll have to fix that.

Chapter Nine

For a moment, Claire got lost in his dark brown eyes. She sat so close to him if she leaned in she could brush her lips against his.

Surprised at herself, she lept to her feet, heart racing. Where had those thoughts come from? The heat flooded her cheeks.

"Are you alright?" Haden reached out to steady her. "You jumped like something pinched you."

"No! no, I'm fine. I remembered… a letter I meant to give you the other day and had forgotten about it… until I saw the mail today." Claire hurried around her desk to put some distance between them. "It's here."

She rummaged through the top drawer and pulled out an official looking envelope. "I wasn't sure what to do with it, and you were on the phone."

"No problem," Haden opened the envelope and studied the contents. "It's an invitation to the Businessman's Annual Charity Ball."

"Oh, I've heard of that. The Chamber of Commerce and the Business League put it together as a way to raise funds for local charities. When is it?"

"Says here, it's next Friday, but the invitations tend to come out a solid month before the event." Haden flipped the envelope over and looked at the post mark. "Oh, it went to the wrong address. No wonder, I got it late."

Claire fought the impulse to lean in for a closer look.

"I'm sure me hiding it in the top drawer for a few days didn't help. Are you thinking about going?"

"Yeah, I'm the newest member of the board for the Business League, so it's expected." Haden cut his eyes towards Claire. "I don't suppose you'd like to go with me?"

"It depends. Are we doing the dating thing or are we making things up as we go?"

Haden tapped the invitation on his knee. "Well, we can either make it up and keep each other informed of the particulars, which seems like a lot of work."

"Yeah, and what if you say one thing and I say another. It could get messy. Adele and your mom are pretty sharp, and as we've found out, they talk on a regular basis."

"Exactly. Or we can go out, so we'll be sure to have our facts straight." Haden leaned across the desk, drawing closer to Claire, and whispered, "It could be fun."

At the drop of his voice, Claire's stomach fluttered.

"Let me think about."

"Alright, but I'll need to know by three. I have to get my R.S.V.P. over to Carol at the Chamber of Commerce before the end of the day. I should've had it in last week."

"I know. Sorry. I'll let you know by three." Claire sat back in her chair and pulled out her keyboard. She started typing some invoices, turning her back to him. She needed him to leave, so she could think.

He didn't.

Instead, he sat for a moment watching her, holding the invitation.

Did he regret inviting her? The longer he sat, the louder the doubts and questions grew.

At last, Haden stood and sauntered down the hall to his office.

Her mind whirled.

It had been so long since any man had shown interest in her. She'd shut the door on that part of her life years ago when Ryan left.

Now, Haden offered companionship without any pretense or misguided expectations because it wouldn't be real. They'd put on a performance for the sake of his mother.

A simple act.

Her heart dropped as the wave of disappointment meandered its way through her thoughts and mingling with her desire.

∞

Claire knew her decision had been the right one, but it didn't keep her from playing the 'what if' game. She let her mind formulate the questions as she walked towards City Hall to turn in the invitation to Carol White. The warm April breeze played with her hair.

What if I said yes? What's the worst that could happen? She followed her questions to their possible answers. I could get fired, be back to job hunting again. Or I could have a good time. I could enjoy Haden's company and want to see more of him. We could date for real and maybe, find… Her thoughts refused to move forward in the game.

She looked at the RSVP card in her hand. It would have been so easy to check the plus one box. But no, she let her practical side dictate her path.

Haden hadn't liked her decision. His furrowed brow and deep

scowl told her his thoughts on the matter.

Claire climbed the stairs to the glass doors which opened up into the hallway of the second floor of City Hall. She didn't know which of these doors led to the Chamber of Commerce, so she began reading the plaques beside them.

One of the doors a few feet away flew open and out stormed Sarah accompanied by a lady with salt and pepper hair, wearing orthopedic shoes. Her badges gave her the air of being in charge. "Look, Miss Dempsey, I know this is important to you, but no one knew you would be here this soon. Your architecture firm wasn't even expecting you till after the event."

"Surely, it can't be this hard to get an invitation to the Businessman's Annual Charity ball? I mean, what's the big deal?" The well-dressed Sarah crossed her arms, wrinkling her linen jacket.

The lady raised her chin. "The big deal, as you put it, is that we have already given the caterers a solid number for dinner. We counted our guest list with all their plus ones. So, your options are to miss the event or get someone to invite as their plus one."

Sarah puckered her lips like she had eaten a sour grape and gave the lady a hard stare. The woman didn't flinch. Neither gave way until Sarah pivoted and marched toward the glass doors.

Once Sarah was out of earshot, the lady turned to Claire. "Can I help you?"

"I was here to turn in an RSVP card for my employer," she said.

"Oh, come on in. I'll need my list to verify everything." Opening the door, the lady turned on a dime in her orthopedic shoes and squished her way across the carpeted waiting area to a desk in the back.

"I hope I'm not too late. My employer, Haden Sawyer, had a family…thing this week and so did I." She fidgeted with the card in her hand, nervous as if she were in the principal's office.

"It should be alright." The lady looked up and surveyed Claire. "You said you work for Haden Sawyer, right?"

"Yes."

"Are you by any chance Claire?"

"Yes, I am." Claire not knowing what to do, presented the card to the lady. "May I ask who you are?"

"Oh, I'm sorry. How rude of me. I'm Carol White." After taking the card, Carol extended her hand, and Claire shook it. "I've known Haden since he was knee-high. Adele and Betty and I go way back." A smile spread across the wrinkles which laid around her mouth.

The clouds lifted, and Claire understood why Carol had known who she was.

"They have so many good things to say about you, and I understand you have a son." Carol looked down at the card she now held, and the smile faded.

"Yes, that's right." Claire leaned forward a bit to see what had caused Carol's sullen look.

"This can't be right. There's no plus one. Aren't you going with Haden to the Businessman's Ball? Everyone will be there. It's one of the town's biggest events."

Claire paled. She didn't know what to say, but before her brain caught up to her mouth, she sputtered, "My son has a medical condition, and I don't feel comfortable leaving him with someone new."

"Don't be silly. Adele or Betty would love to sit for you. It would be the highlight of their year."

"I don't want to impose on them. Besides with Betty ill, it wouldn't be right."

"Well, if that's the case, there's always Kyle or Jed. I'm sure they could manage for one evening." Claire could see Carol was not one to be deterred.

"I'm sorry, Carol, but I wouldn't feel comfortable going out and leaving Henry."

"Oh, is that your son's name? Henry? Isn't that funny. That was old man Sawyer's name."

"Haden told me." Claire smiled, then made a big display of noticing the clock on the wall behind Carol's desk. "Oh goodness. I've got to get back and finish up a few things before I have to go and pick up Henry from Mrs. Nolen's."

"Oh, you have Henry at Mrs. Nolen's Bright Starts Daycare. Good choice."

"Well, that's the price us single parents pay – childcare." Claire waved as she made a beeline for the door.

Once outside the office, she leaned against the wall to let her heart stop jumping around. This cannot be good. Now, they've got me telling lies. A groan slipped out before she could catch it, and the man passing by looked back at her.

It's like murder, and I'm an accomplice.

∞

"Betty, are you in the living room?" Adele's voice rang loud against the quiet of her sister-in-law's house. She had let herself in the back door that leads into the kitchen, so she could place the plastic container of hot soup on the counter.

Betty and Adele had been backdoor buddies since Adele moved to Miller Creek after her husband's death. It seemed so long ago. Kyle had been a toddler, and now, twenty years later, he was a man. She owed so much to Betty and Otis for their help in raising her son.

"In here." Betty called. Adele followed the sound into the little office off the main entrance.

"What are you doing in here? You should be resting."

"There will be time enough for that once I'm six feet under." Betty looked up from the computer, grinning.

Adele ignored it. Betty's attempt at humor left her cold. Her dear friend and sister-in-law was battling breast cancer. Adele wrestled every day with her own emotions about the situation. They had both lost their husbands; she didn't want to lose her best friend.

"Oh, don't be an old stick in the mud. You know as well as I do breast cancer if caught early can be handled. The doctor said Stage II has something like a 93 percent survival rate," said Betty.

"I don't care. After watching Otis." Adele stopped. She didn't want to hurt Betty by dredging up those awful months with Otis, her brother-in-law, sick with lung cancer. At the end, he had fought for every breath he took.

"I know watching Otis was as hard for you as it was for me." Betty pushed herself out of the chair and went to Adele. "I don't know what either one of us would have done without you."

Adele reached out and hugged her sister-in-law; her arms compressed the too large shirt next to Betty's thin frame. "I'm the one grateful. If you and Otis hadn't been willing to help me after Lars died, I don't know what Kyle and I would've done."

"Oh, I'm sure the Lord would have provided some other way."

"Yes, but I'm glad he used you and Otis."

Betty let go of Adele and sat on the love seat which ran along the wall adjacent to the desk. She patted the spot beside her. Adele curled her feet up under her as she snuggled into a comfortable position. "Otis kept Kyle on the straight and narrow and having your boys to traipse around with during those teenage years… well, I know Kyle wouldn't be the man he is without his Uncle Otis."

Betty's eyes filled with tears. They glistened on the rim of her lids. She reached up and swiped them away. "Otis loved Kyle like he was one of his. It gave him such pleasure to know he was doing his best by his brother, Lars. It was his way of honoring his memory."

"I know. And it made all the difference. Kyle needed a man's influence and Otis…" Now, her own eyes filled with tears.

Adele jumped up and grabbed the box of tissues from off the desk, chiding herself for letting all these emotions and memories flood out.

"I'm sorry, Betty. I shouldn't have brought up Otis and the boys and been so squishy."

"No, they're good memories. I wouldn't trade one of them." Betty dabbed at her eyes.

"Me either."

"But I do think I need to focus on the here and now. Keep my mind on today and the near future," said Betty.

"You're right."

The computer fan kicked on making a horrible noise as it came to life. Adele decided to use the distraction to change the subject. "What were you doing when I came in? Getting everything in order; paying up the bills?"

"No, but that's not a bad idea." Betty got up and went back over to the computer. "I was being a little angel of love."

"Oh, playing Cupid again. Does this have anything to do with our present love project?" Adele wiggled her eyebrows.

"Yes, as a matter of fact, it does. I talked with Carol White today, and she had some very interesting information about the potential couple."

"Are you going to share?"

"Of course, I'm going to share. I can't do this without your expertise. After all, you're the one known for your matchmaking. I'm a beginner."

"So, what did Carol tell you."

Betty sat at the desk and scrolled down the screen with the mouse. "She sent me an email about Claire and Sarah. Okay, here it is."

"Claire and Sarah? I don't follow."

"Hold on. According to Carol, Sarah came in to her office today wanting a ticket to the Businessman's Ball. The hospital hadn't expected her to arrive to work on the renovations until later in May. So, neither the hospital nor the architecture firm she's working for had put her on their invite list."

"Oh, so she doesn't have an invitation."

"Exactly. Which might work to our advantage in getting Claire and Haden together."

"How?" Adele didn't see the connection.

"Well, and this is the underhanded, tricky part. In order for Sarah to go to the ball, she'll need to go with someone as their plus one. I'm thinking about planting the bug in her ear about Haden needing a date."

"Isn't Claire going with him?"

"No, she isn't. Carol said when Claire dropped off the RSVP card there was no plus one. She even asked her about it, and Claire gave her an excuse about not wanting to leave Henry with anyone new. So, Haden is going alone."

"That is interesting," said Adele. "So, by giving Sarah the idea about going with Haden, you will force Haden to take Claire. What if she won't go?"

"Well, they're pretty deep into this 'Mom, meet my girlfriend' fabrication. So, I'll simply mention how strange it is they're not going together and that I'm sure Claire wouldn't mind if he goes with Sarah, as old friends."

"That is a bit underhanded. I'm not sure we should do it. If Haden finds out you suggested the idea to Sarah, he'll blow a gasket." Adele stretched her legs out and propped her back against the arm of the love seat.

"Yeah, I know." Betty bit her lip. "But Claire and Haden looked so cute together, yesterday, standing there holding hands. Besides, I want grandchildren before I'm too old to enjoy them. How does the saying go 'desperate times call for desperate measures'?"

"Here, here," echoed Adele. "Grandchildren or bust. From what you said happened at the hospital, there is no way Haden is going to the ball with Sarah, not even for a minute."

"That's what I'm counting on. Haden can be very persuasive when he wants to be. All he'll have to do is tell Claire if she doesn't go he'll be pushed into going with Sarah. Of course, I'll be the one applying the pressure. Claire is bound to save him from that fate."

"What makes you think she will? I know for a fact she isn't comfortable about having lied to you, and now since others know, she may want to come clean. Why do you think she'll rescue Haden again?" Adele asked.

"Because there's an attraction between them. They beam when they're together, and I know for certain she doesn't like Sarah's attitude. You should've seen the look on her face when Sarah kissed Haden, as big as you please on the cheeks, not caring if Claire was his girlfriend or not."

"Umm, jealous." Adele said.

"Oh yeah," Betty nodded. "She'll come to his rescue. Now, we need to make sure Cinderella Claire goes to the ball."

With those words, Betty got a strange look in her eyes as she tilted her head and swept her gaze over Adele.

"I think it's time to go eat the soup I brought." Adele threw her legs over the edge of the love seat about to stand and make her escape.

"Hold on a minute, do you still have that dress Wendy gave you? The pretty blue one?"

"Yeah, she wanted me to hold on to it. Said it was too puffy to fit in her closet at her apartment, and her waitress uniforms make everything smell like day old French fries."

Betty raised her eyebrows and tapped her finger on her chin. "Do you think it would fit Claire?"

"Maybe, they're about the same size. Why?" Adele could see Betty's wheels turning.

Betty wiggled her eyebrows and replied, "Because my dear friend, if I'm Cupid, you're the Fairy Godmother."

Chapter Ten

The rain began to come down in earnest sometime around two o'clock. The gray shadows crept across the floor of the small trailer, making the office cool even for spring. Claire jumped at the clap of thunder, the rumble shaking the glass in the tiny window of the door.

What a dreary Friday. Claire leaned against the door and watched the rain. The clatter on the roof made it hard for her to concentrate on her work.

As she turned to move away from the window, Jed drove up.

His truck splashed through a puddle and pulled to a stop within inches of the stairs. He emerged from the cab holding a yellow rain jacket above his head with one hand and a stack of papers in the other. Hands full, he kicked his truck door shut.

Claire grabbed the doorknob and swung the stubborn door out. Jed dashed for the opening as Claire stepped back to give the long-legged man room. Another roll of thunder sounded through the space.

Jed dropped the rain jacket and slammed the door behind him. He flung his head and shoulders like an old golden retriever. "What a mess,"

"I'll take those for you." Claire took the papers from Jed's hand, depositing them on her desk.

"Why, thank you. You wouldn't happen to have a towel lying around, here would you?"

"No but let me get you some paper towels."

Claire dug around in the kitchen pantry and returned with a half-used roll. Jed took it and tore off several small white squares. Pressing them to his shirt, the towels became soggy and tore, leaving behind a trail of lint glued to his black tee-shirt.

Claire grinned at his antics.

"Not helping much, is it?" Jed winked in her direction while he patted his jeans with another handful of paper towels.

"No, not really."

Jed gave up the attempt, tossing the wilted squares into the trash.

Claire moved towards her chair but stopped. The thought struck her that Jed, in his wet jeans and all, might take his usual seat on the edge of her desk.

"Let me go get you a chair out of Haden's office." Claire offered.

"That'd be great. I suppose you don't want a drowned rat dripping all over your nice, dry desk." The twinkle of mischief in Jed's eyes was unmistakable. He enjoyed teasing her.

"No, I certainly do not."

Claire liked Jed, but Haden, he made her heart race. She hadn't seen much of him in the last two days, ever since she told him no to accompanying him to the Businessman's Charity Ball.

"Where's the old man?" called Jed as Claire carried the aluminum framed chair down the hall. "Oh, let me help you." Jed met Claire at the end of the narrow hallway and took the chair from her.

"Old man? Aren't you the oldest Sawyer?"

"Yeah, but Haden acts like he's the grandpa. He's too consumed with the business. I don't remember the last time he went out and had some plain ole fun." Jed set the chair down in front of Claire's desk and took a seat. Crossing his legs at the ankles, he leaned back.

Claire settled into her seat. She sensed Jed was working up to something, but she had no idea what.

"Did you happen to send in the RSVP for the Businessman's Charity Ball?"

Oh, so this was about the Charity Ball. She figured he wanted to know why she wasn't going with Haden. "Yes, I walked it over to Carol White on Wednesday. Haden didn't want to take a chance of missing the deadline, and since I was late in giving it to him…"

"You walked it over," finished Jed.

"Yeah." Claire opened one of the files on her desk and began to skim it. She didn't want to have this conversation with Jed. He should know better than anyone how uncomfortable she was with the lie she and Haden told. She flat out refused to contribute to it by going to the ball.

Jed sat quiet for a moment. "I kind of ran into Carol White today over at City Hall."

Claire raised her eyes from the file to read Jed's expression. She braced herself. "Great."

Jed leaned forward and inspected his work boots.

Claire set the file aside. "Look Jed, it's obvious you've got something on your mind, so spit it out."

"Alright," Jed straightened. "I wanted to know since you aren't going with Haden if you'd go with me?"

Claire sat stunned. It took her a moment to process what he had said.

Jed had treated her for the most part like a kid sister, goofing off, making jokes. There had been nothing to indicate he had any romantic feelings for her. Okay, maybe he hung around a little too often, but it had always been playful banter and pal type stuff.

"I'm flattered, but you know I can't. Your mom thinks I'm dating Haden." Claire hoped this answer would satisfy him. She struggled against the frustration she felt. Jed, who knew the truth about her and Haden, sat here acting like a love-sick teen.

She didn't need him to cause any more complications.

"Okay, let me ask you this. If Mom didn't think you were dating Haden, would you go with me?" Claire reached up and played with her ponytail, twirling it between her fingers.

"That's okay. I see." Jed kept his eyes on his boots.

"You know you're one of my favorite people." Claire looked across her desk, willing Jed to lift his eyes.

"But not the favorite."

"Right now, Henry is the favorite. I haven't had time for dating or any kind of love life in years. With Henry's medical issues, I don't know when I will. My last official date was with my ex-husband, Ryan. And that was years ago."

"That's a shame. You're a sweet lady with plenty to give the right guy." Now, Jed met her gaze. She hated the hurt she saw there. Jed pushed his hands against his knees and stood. "I better get going. The Thomas site is down to the sheet rocking and trim painting. I'll need to go over and check the crew's progress. The paperwork for the materials on the Henderson project is in the red file folder."

Jed grabbed his rain jacket. As he reached the door, he paused with his hand on the knob, his voice even toned. "I don't think your refusal has anything to do with Henry. I've seen how you act when Haden enters the room. You light up."

"Jed, you're so wrong. It's Henry."

"I don't think so." Jed adjusted his stance. Claire met his stare. "You can keep telling yourself that, but whatever you believe, make sure Haden doesn't get hurt. His heart's been damaged by one woman. That's enough."

Jed slammed the door, leaving Claire to her thoughts. The thunder groaned miles away, sending gentle ripples through the spring air.

The mention of Haden's name caused Claire's heart to flutter. She lifted her hand and felt the heat radiating from her face.

"This is ridiculous," she muttered to herself. "Who's the teenager now?"

∞

Adele had been preoccupied all day. When the rain started, her customer flow slowed to a crawl, giving her more time to think.

With two coffee drinkers at the counter as her sole customers, she decided to take a break. "Frank, I'll be sitting in the front booth by the cash register if you need me."

Frank hunched over and poked his gray haired, head through the pick-up window. He dinged the bell. "I've got you covered, sweet thing." He winked.

Adele waved him off. "If you'd put half as much time into your cooking as you do your flattering, you'd be a millionaire chef by now."

"Oh, I can see my name in lights. 'Frank the Tank'" Adele knew Tank was the nickname his army buddies had given him back in Vietnam.

"I can see it too, and you might need a different name for your restaurant. You wouldn't want people to say 'let's go eat at the tank.' Would you?"

"I don't know, if it fits, why not?" Frank shrugged his broad shoulders and disappeared back into his world of the kitchen.

Adele stopped to fix herself a cup of coffee. Her head ached. All morning, she'd been trying to figure out how to help Betty with their matchmaking project.

They had both agreed not to mention anything to Sarah about Haden going to the ball unattached. It seemed too cruel to do that to him. He had been through enough with that woman, and from what he told Betty, he was now in a good place, ready to move on. Which put Claire in the right place at the right time, she'd say.

Adele grinned to herself as she thought about the first time she met Claire. It was over a year ago. The woman was a mess, but still, she saw the potential. But, it wasn't the right time for either of them. Then, the Lord brought Claire in bemoaning the loss of another job, and Jed happened in. Beautiful.

Adele walked over to the front booth and slid into the seat facing the door and the cash register. She held the mug in both hands, letting the warmth radiate through her as she took a sip.

Betty had given her the task of getting Haden and Claire to the family Sunday dinner. Easier said than done. Adele took another sip of her mental grease.

She closed her eyes against the throbbing in her head and prayed. *Lord, I know how you feel about the whole lying thing, and I know how you hate buts. But…please use this situation for Haden and Claire's good even if they're going about it backwards. Be with Betty; give her doctors wisdom and guidance. I need her, Lord.*

The doorbell jingled, and Adele sang out, "Welcome to Adele's Café. Take a seat, and I'll be right with you." She started to pull herself out of the booth.

"No rush, Aunt Adele." She stopped short of standing as Jed walked over to where she sat. He slid into the seat across from her, plopping his elbows on the table, and planting his chin in his hands. His sandy blonde hair damp from the rain.

"Something wrong?"

"You could say that."

"Okay, do you think a cup of coffee or a plate of fries might help to fix the issue?"

"Maybe, but I think it'll take more than fries to fix my hurt ego."

"Oh, girl trouble? Well, I don't know of anything that mends the pride, except time and humility."

Jed groaned and leaned back in the booth. "Aunt Adele, I know what I want in life, and it never gets around to being my turn to go for it, but others get two or three turns."

"Don't say it." Adele held her hands up. "Life isn't fair, and never will be. However, life can be good, and from my point of view, your life is pretty good. You've got a job, a home, a family who loves you."

"I know I should be grateful, but I'm…I don't know. I want more."

Adele reached out and patted his hand. "I know you do, honey, but be patient. Your time will come. God knows the perfect time for the next season in your life."

Jed sighed. Adele hated to see him so dejected.

"How about a piece of apple pie, my treat." Adele stood and walked over to the counter where the pie case sat. She cut him a piece.

Returning, she slid the piece in front of him. "Here you go, sweetie."

The doorbell jingled, and Adele looked up to see who it was before singing out her traditional greeting. She found Claire standing in the doorway drenched, wrestling with her umbrella.

"Hi Claire, I didn't expect to see you today. You must be starved if you got out in this nasty weather. What can I get for you?"

"I was hoping for a hot cup of coffee and maybe a burger. I forgot to pack a lunch." Claire said as she finished pulling the strap around her umbrella.

Jed turned around in his seat as Claire looked up.

Adele couldn't miss the look that passed between them.

"Oh, I…um… I…think I'll sit at the counter."

"I need to be going. Thanks for the pie, Aunt Adele." Jed rose from the booth and kissed Adele on the top of her head. "I'll see you Sunday at Mom's, right?"

Adele perked up at the mention of Sunday. "I'll be there with bells on."

"Good, Mom needs all the family time she can get, right now." Jed passed by Claire, cutting his eyes her way as he pushed the door open.

Adele figured the glare had something to do with the fairness of life.

"Was it me, or is there something going on between you two?"

"I'm pretty sure I hurt his feelings, but I can't help that."

"Well, don't fret. I'm sure it'll all work out."

Claire let out a sigh and followed Adele to the counter where she ordered a bacon cheeseburger and fries along with a hot cup of coffee.

The order came up quick due to the lack of customers, and Adele took advantage of the opportunity to find out some information. "So, since everyone thinks you and Haden are dating, I suppose you two will be going to the Businessman's Charity Ball next Friday night? Are you excited? What do you plan to wear?"

Claire's face fell. She looked like a puppy caught doing something wrong. The guilt dripped off her. "I'm not going. I don't want to leave Henry with someone new."

"Oh, well, you could let Betty watch him." Adele stopped for a moment. "No, she's not up to it at least not alone, and I'll be at the Businessmen's ball myself. Rats."

Claire's shoulders wilted. "Okay, I have to tell you something."

Claire looked around. Leaning forward, she lowered her voice. "Jed asked me to go to the ball, but I said no because of this terrible lie which made him mad." The words flooded out of her. "Then he accused me of having feelings for Haden which of course is absurd."

With this admission, Claire's complexion reddened. "I've gotten myself into a hole all because I wanted to help Haden." Claire bit down hard on the bacon cheeseburger in her hand.

"Whoa, girl. Slow down. It's going to be alright."

"No, it's not. I hate lying to everyone like this. I'm torn. I don't want to disappoint his mom, but I know what's right and that's supposed to mean something." She again attacked the burger.

Adele arranged the plastic water glasses, thinking through what she wanted to say. "Okay, sweetie. First, Haden is the one who told the lie. You were just helping a friend. And second, is Jed, right?"

Claire swallowed the bite in her mouth. "What do you mean?"

"Do you have feelings for Haden?"

"I do respect him, and he can be very sweet." Claire's face lit up as she began talking about him. "He brings me coffee every morning he's in the office. And he does have the deepest brown eyes I've ever seen on anyone. It's like wading in pools of chocolate when he looks at me." Claire stopped. "I mean they're so warm." She picked up some fries and jammed them into her mouth.

Adele had her answer.

"Umm. Well, in that case, I would advise you to do what Haden asked to begin with and follow his lead."

"He wants me to keep pretending for his mother's sake."

"Okay, do it, and since that's what's happening, I'm going to invite you to come to Betty's house on Sunday for our family dinner. If she thinks you and Haden are dating, she'll expect to see you there."

"What if Haden doesn't want me there?'

"Why wouldn't he want you there? Isn't he the one who won't own up to the truth?"

"He's been avoiding me. He suggested we do a few things together so we could keep our story straight and asked me to the Businessman's

Charity Ball."

"Which I hear you declined." Adele shook her head. "It's his pride that's hurt. That's all. He'll come around."

"How did I get into this mess." Claire groaned, leaning her head into both her hands. "One brother asking me out, another telling their mom I'm his girlfriend. Plus, half the town thinks we're dating, and now, the guy I'm pretending to date is mad at me. This is more complicated than a real relationship."

Adele suppressed a laugh. Claire had the kind of problems most women loved having, too many interested men. "Listen here, you plan to show up at Betty's. She'll be expecting you and Henry after church. I'll take care of that hard-headed nephew of mine."

Frank stuck his head out the pick-up window. "Yeah, Adele can handle the Sawyer men. She's been doing it for years."

Yes, she had but getting Haden to be nice to Claire at Sunday lunch was one thing, getting him to ask her to the Charity Ball a second time. Now that, that was a challenge.

∞

Adele entered Betty's kitchen through the back door. She placed the take-out containers from the China Palace on the kitchen island before depositing the ice cream she had confiscated from the café into the freezer.

The air filled with the smells of sweet and sour chicken, moo Shu shrimp and Adele's favorite chicken lo mein. Betty had called her and requested dinner from the China Palace. So, Adele dropped everything and made the run, leaving Frank, Cherie, and the new girl Carly to handle the Friday dinner rush.

When Adele turned around, she found Betty sitting at the kitchen table working a crossword puzzle. It bothered her how tired Betty had been lately. She noticed the dark circles under her eyes, and how she sat more often. Worry started to set in. She busied herself to ward it off.

"How are you feeling today?" Adele went to the cabinet to the right of the stove and pulled down two plates.

"Tired, but that's the new normal. Other than that, I don't even know I'm sick."

Cancer's funny that way, thought Adele. "What do you want to drink?"

"Uh, I don't know. Surprise me." Betty set her crossword to one side.

Adele fished around in the refrigerator and decided cola would go best with Chinese food. She poured the drinks and set Betty's in front of her. "Do you want a little of everything or a lot of the sweet and sour chicken?" She raised an eyebrow.

Betty grinned up at her with a twinkle in her eye. "I suppose I'll take a lot of the sweet and sour chicken if you don't mind. Extra sauce on the side."

"I thought you might say that. I got two tubs of the sauce."

Adele dished the food onto the plates and took a seat next to Betty

After saying grace, Adele plunged into the matter occupying her mind. "I saw Claire today."

"Oh, and how is she and Haden getting along? Has there been any progress in getting Cinder Claire to the ball?" Betty stabbed a rather slippery piece of chicken then soaked it in the tub of sweet and sour sauce.

"Not any towards the ball, but I did get her to agree to come to Sunday lunch." Adele twirled the lo mien onto her fork. "She didn't think Haden would want her here, though, and that might be cause for concern."

"Why would she think that?" Betty's brows furrowed.

"She said he's been avoiding her ever since she turned down his invitation. I think his pride is wounded."

"Sounds like it." Betty answered.

"And on top of that, Jed asked her to the ball." Adele took a bite.

"Jed? How did he get in the mix?" Betty shook her head. "That's not good. What did she say to him?"

Adele sipped her drink. "No. Same as she told Haden." She put her fork down. "You should've seen him. He dragged into the café looking like a scolded puppy with his ears hanging low. I felt so sorry for him. He's such a wonderful young man. But Claire's not the one for him."

"Are we sure about that? Would you stake your matchmaking reputation on it?" Betty's eyes cut through her.

"Yes, I would," Adele assured her. "Claire's the right one for Haden. I knew it the minute I met her. Haden needs a woman who can be his equal, and she needs a husband to help raise that sweet boy of hers. I don't care if they are too short-sighted to see it. We're simply placing the spotlight on what everybody else in town can see so plainly."

"Everyone but Jed." Betty took a sip of her cola and leaned back. She grew quiet.

Adele ate a few bites and waited. Finally, she asked, "What are you thinking? I can hear the gears grinding from here."

Betty sat up and leaned her arms on the table. "I think we need to take some drastic steps."

"No, no, no. Betty Sawyer, I see that look in your eye, and it's only gonna cause more trouble." Adele shook her head and crossed her arms. "We agreed. We wouldn't use Sarah."

"Now, hear me out."

"No, we can't do that to Haden. You can't do that to Haden, you're his mother." Adele held her hand up and turned her face. "If he finds out, he'll never forgive us."

"Look, we're running out of time. We have less than a week to get Claire and Haden to agree to go to the ball together. They have to go. It's the perfect setting for two people to fall in love. I just know it'll seal the deal."

Adele stared at Betty not sure what to say. She agreed they were running out of time, but this?

"Besides, we don't have to be the ones to do it," continued Betty. "We can ask Carol White over at the Chamber of Commerce to mention it to Sarah that Haden needs a date. We all know how bad Sarah wants to go to this event, and she needs to be someone's plus one. It's perfect."

A twinge of guilt crept over Adele. This plan did call for some extreme measures. But Claire could be stubborn, and Haden couldn't see what was standing right in front of him. And Jed, well, he compounded the problem.

"I just hope we're doing the right thing," Adele placed her elbows on the table and laced her fingers together. "So, where do we start?"

"I'll email Carol, tonight." Betty beamed with excitement. Adele wasn't use to being the reluctant one when it came to matchmaking.

"Do you think she'll mind helping?" Adele asked.

"She'll be thrilled. Don't let her practical orthopedic shoes fool you, she an old romantic at heart. She'd do anything for love."

"How are we going to make sure Claire intervenes and saves Haden from Sarah. Or what if Sarah talks Haden into going and Claire never gets a chance to change her mind?" Adele frowned. "I don't like it. There's too many loose ends."

"Hmm…you said Claire had agreed to come to Sunday lunch, right?" Betty pursed her lips and tapped her finger on them.

"Yeah, oh great mastermind of love."

"Then let's make sure Sarah is here, too. That way they'll all be together when Sarah asks Haden to take her." Betty winked.

"That might work. Once Claire sees Sarah on the prowl, she'll go." Relief flooded Adele. At least this way, she'd be here to pick up the pieces if anything should go wrong.

"You bet she will, and you'll need to be ready with your Fairy Godmother magic. That's why I asked you about Wendy's dress. In case, there isn't much time."

Adele stood and went to the counter for a pen and paper. She found what she needed in one of the drawers and returned to the table. "I better start a list. I'll need to check out the Shoe Source to see if I can find something to match. I'd hate to do all this 'magic' and her have to go to the ball barefooted."

"She'll need a purse or something to carry her phone." Betty added.

Adele jotted it down. "I might need to pick up some stockings, too."

Betty heaved a sigh. "Haden deserves some happiness in his life. I know we all hope things go our way with this surgery, and I'm sure it will, but I'm not going to be around forever." Betty looked over at Adele. "I just want my guys to have someone the way we did Adele."

"I know, Betty. Those Sawyer brothers were some good men. We were blessed to have them for as long as we did."

Betty reached out and took her sister-in-law's hand. "Adele, I don't know what I would've done without you here when Otis got sick. Now, here you are again."

Adele covered their intertwined hands with her other, "You, Betty Sawyer, are my dear friend, and as long as I have breath in me, I'll be right here in your corner." She patted Betty's hand. "Now, eat your sweet and sour chicken before it gets cold. You know it can't stand up to being microwaved."

Chapter Eleven

Shutting off the shower, Haden dried and wrapped the towel around his hips. The hot water had felt good on his tired muscles. He'd spent the early morning hours tossing and turning as he wrestled with how to ask Claire for her help, again. It was the last thing he wanted to do, but there was no getting around it.

Haden padded down the hall in his bare feet and pulled a t-shirt from his drawer as he contemplated his predicament. He slipped it over his shoulders, leaving it lose around the waist. His mother had phoned the night before extending an invitation for him and Claire and "of course her sweet Henry" to come for Sunday dinner.

Her excitement added to the guilt building up inside of him. He wrestled with coming clean, but he didn't dare tell her the truth of the situation over the phone. Though it would've been easier on him, it would've been the coward's way. No, he told the lie in person; he'd set the record straight the same way.

Maybe, inviting Claire to Mom's would give him the chance he needed, but what if she wouldn't come?

He mulled this over as he wandered into the kitchen. The dishes from the previous night sat in the sink. He hated loading the dishwasher. As he grabbed the eggs from the refrigerator, his mind went back over the last few days.

He wanted to kick himself. His pride had kept him away from

Claire. He could still smell the smoke of his invitation being shot down in flames. She'd said no, and he'd let his ego get in his way.

He heard the front door bang closed as he cracked four eggs into the skillet.

"Hey, you up?" Kyle called.

"Yeah, back here in the kitchen." Haden pulled out a second glass and filled it with orange juice.

As Kyle entered, he threw his hat down on the small Formica table "I hadn't been in the office since Tuesday, and I wanted to give you an update. The rain yesterday slowed down the painting progress at the Thomas site by a day or two. Everything else is on schedule."

"Good to know. Juice?" Haden handed Kyle the glass then moved to the stove to scramble the eggs.

"Thanks, Cuz." Kyle pulled one of the chairs out from under the table and angled it.

Haden grabbed the plate of eggs and the juice and joined Kyle at the table.

"So, how's Claire? I hear she has a new boyfriend."

Haden stiffened.

"As far as I know, Claire's fine." Haden moved his eggs around on his plate.

Kyle sat up straight with his brows furrowed. "What do you mean as far as you know? You didn't fire her, did you?"

"No, I didn't fire her." Haden spit-out. "I've been avoiding her."

"Why on earth are you avoiding Claire? First, you tell Aunt Betty she's your girlfriend…"

"Only because Sarah was there. She had me pinned up against the wall with her talking about the good ole days. I thought if there was someone else in the picture she'd leave me alone and move on. I didn't think it all the way through." Haden stabbed at his eggs.

"Do you still care about her?"

"No, I got over her a while back, but it doesn't make it any easier to be around her, and when she started cooing at me and doing those cheek kisses." Haden rolled his eyes. "I was desperate."

"Well, Claire's a good sport, and I'm sure there was no harm done. I know Aunt Betty understood."

"That's the problem. I haven't straightened it out. Mom was so happy when I introduced Claire as my girlfriend. She lit up like a Christmas tree."

"You didn't tell Aunt Betty it was a ruse?"

"No, instead I asked Claire to go along with it until after the surgery."

"Well, I saw Jed yesterday, and he wasn't happy. I think he asked her to go with him to the Businessman's Charity Ball thinking you had cleared things up with your mom."

Haden released a huff and pushed the plate away. "Jed's been hanging around Claire, a lot."

"Yeah, because he likes her, but he told me he got the impression Claire had eyes for someone else."

Haden clenched both of his fists and nailed Kyle with his glare. "Who?"

Kyle's eyebrows raised. "You've got to be kidding me? Don't you know?"

"No, I haven't seen her hanging around with anyone other than Jed."

"And you." Kyle shook his head. "You are thick."

"Me? No, she's mad at me, disappointed I've let things get out of hand with Mom, but there is no way that woman has any other feelings for me except utter annoyance."

"How do you know?"

"Well, I asked her to the Charity Ball, and she turned me down flat. She used Henry's medical condition as the excuse."

"Maybe, it wasn't an excuse. Besides, when you say flat, do you mean she answered no right away, or did she have to think about it for a minute."

"She took a couple of hours, but then it was a flat no."

Kyle groaned, set his empty glass on the table, and picked up his hat. "You, my friend, are an idiot."

Placing his hat on his head, Kyle stood.

"What? I know I'm right," called Haden as he watched Kyle stride through the living room to the front door. "If Claire Reed has any feelings for me, I'll eat that last cigar in my Dad's stash."

"You mean the Cuban one he was saving for their Fiftieth Anniversary?"

"Yep."

Kyle stopped at the door, and turned, "Deal."

∞

Haden sat at his desk. The muscles in his shoulders tensed as he listened to Claire's movements in the outer room. He waited half expecting her to appear in his doorway with a greeting or a contract or some little something she'd forgotten to get him to sign. However, to his disappointment, she didn't.

After thirty minutes of letting his mind drift between his computer screen and the door, he scolded himself. "Get a grip," Trying to take his own advice, he turned his attention to the pages laying sprawled out before him.

Once focused on his work, he lost himself in it.

"Haden. Haden." Claire called from the doorway holding a clipboard in her left hand and a sticky note in her right. "Haden are you listening?"

Looking up, he answered. "Oh, sorry Claire, I didn't…" He began to explain but decided against it. "What do you need?" He asked instead.

"Your mom called about half an hour ago. She didn't want me to disturb you, so I took a message, but I thought you needed to see it."

Claire walked forward to give Haden the sticky note. He held out his hand to receive it, but she hesitated, pressing her lips together.

"I don't bite." His irritation seeped out in his words.

"I know you don't." Claire squared her shoulders and slapped the note onto his computer screen, beating a hasty retreat back to her desk.

Haden jerked the note off the screen. It read:

Can't wait to see you and Claire and Henry tomorrow.

It should be loads of fun.

Love Mom.

Haden groaned and sank back in his chair. Great, just great. Now how was he supposed to enlist her help.

He decided it would be better to face Claire head on. No sense in prolonging his agony until the end of the day. Besides, he wouldn't last that long. He wanted to talk to her; shoot, he wanted to hold her and tell her it'd be all right. But if she wouldn't hand him a sticky note, that wasn't happening.

"Claire, we need to talk." His voice sounded gruff even to him.

Claire spun her chair around and faced him. "I'm all ears."

Her words sounded friendly, but her body language sent a different message. Her arms and legs were crossed, and her head was tilted to the side.

He held up the blue sticky note. "What do you want to do about this?"

"What can I do about it? As long as you refuse to straighten out this mess, I guess I'm at your mercy."

Haden leaned his torso against the doorjamb. "I heard Jed asked you to the Businessman's Charity Ball. Do you want to go with him?" He hadn't planned on asking her this, but somewhere deep inside of him, he needed to know her answer. Jed was a great guy, easy to love. He wouldn't blame her for having feelings for him.

"He did ask me, but I told him I couldn't because I didn't want to get someone new to watch Henry."

"Is that the only reason you told him no?" Haden inspected his boots as he waited for her to answer.

"It's one of the reasons. Leaving Henry with someone isn't like leaving most kids with a sitter. They need to know about his medications, and what he can eat that won't give him a stomach ache. His immune system is so low; it makes it tricky." When Haden looked up, worry had clouded Claire's face.

"How is Henry?"

"He has his good days and his bad. The fact he hasn't grown in a few months is disturbing. The doctors are keeping a close eye on him." Claire fiddled with a pen on her desk.

"Oh, does his condition keep him from growing?"

"It can." Her lips drew in, pinched like a bow.

Haden knew he had shown his ignorance on the subject. His own emotions over seeing Sarah had kept him from giving any thought to the havoc he had caused in Claire's life with his lie.

"If you want to go to the Businessman's Charity Ball with Jed, I'll clear everything up with Mom tomorrow." Haden's heart struggled with the idea of Jed holding Claire close while they danced. He'd have to shake it off. She'd made her choice.

"I do want you to clear this up, but I'm not planning on going with anyone to the Charity Ball. I meant what I told you when you hired me. I don't have time or energy for any other man in my life. Henry's it."

Haden nodded and stood to his full height. "Will you go with me to Mom's tomorrow after church?" He held up the sticky note. "As you know, she's expecting you."

"So, I've heard." Claire's strawberry red lips curved into a gentle smile. "Yeah, I'll go. Besides, I already told Adele I would."

"Adele asked you about going to Mom's." Haden frowned.

"Uh-huh, she's as concerned about your mom as you are. But we've got to get this straightened out before it grows any bigger. Your mom has already told half the town about us dating, and who knows who else Sarah and Adele have told."

Haden crumpled up the note and moved towards the desk to throw it into the trash can. "You're right. I should've told Mom the minute Sarah left. I didn't think about how this would affect your life." Haden met her gaze. "I'm sorry for all this."

"It's alright," answered Claire as she reached out and took Haden's hand giving it a squeeze. "What are fake boyfriends for if not to make life messy." Now, Claire was looking up at him with her sparkling green eyes, and a smile wrapped in her red lips, holding his hand.

Haden's mind whirled as his eyes ran from her face to their intertwined hands and returned to her lips.

An overwhelming urge drew him forward. He wanted to kiss those sweet red lips. He needed to find out if they tasted like summer ripe strawberries.

Chapter Twelve

Claire closed her eyes in anticipation. The warmth of Haden's breath on her cheek sent chills down her arms. She had often wondered what a kiss from him would be like.

"Anybody home?" Kyle's voice rang out as the office door banged against the side of the trailer.

Claire pulled her hand from Haden's and jumped back almost falling out of her seat. She shot Haden a warning glance, causing him to chuckle. "Hi Kyle, what can we do for you?"

Claire swiveled her chair to face Kyle, but there was no hiding the heat that rose in her cheeks.

Kyle looked from Claire to Haden. "Am I interrupting something? I get the feeling I am."

"No, no. We were going over a plan… about what to do about… a note." Claire left it at that and turned her attention to her computer screen. Her fingers flew over the keyboard, ignoring both men.

Out of the corner of her eye, she caught Kyle exchanging shrugs with Haden. "What do you need, Kyle?"

"I wanted to talk to you about the Henderson place. How do you want to handle the basement issue? I have a couple of ideas, but I wanted to run them by you to see what you thought."

"Great. The plans are in my office. Why don't you head back; I'll be right behind you."

As Kyle moved out of earshot, Claire turned to find Haden bracing his hands on the desk, leaning in closer to her.

"We can finish this later." Haden's voice held a husky timber.

She shook her head. "I think we've said everything. We both agree we need to straighten this mess out, and tomorrow is the day."

Haden stood up and crossed his arms, grinning down at her.

"What's so funny?" She sputtered.

"Nothing," he said as his grin engulfed his face, allowing his dimples to emerge. "I didn't figure you for a scaredy-cat. That's all."

"A scaredy-cat?" She popped up, pushing her chair out from under her and leaned across her desk, bracing herself with her hands, mimicking his earlier actions. "You think I'm scared of whatever it is going on here? You are so full of yourself. I don't know what you think is happening, but let me tell you, Haden Sawyer, you…you…,"

"Oh, my," he leaned across the desk, meeting her in the middle. "I've never left a woman speechless before, and to think, I didn't even get to the good part yet," and with that, he kissed her.

His kiss was sweet and soft, and Claire soaked it in. Her eyes fluttered close, and she relaxed into it. When they broke apart, Haden lifted his hand and touched her hair, and Claire leaned her head into his palm. A slight moan escaped her lips before Haden kissed her again.

When he pulled away the second time, her lips felt cold.

"I better go see what Kyle needs." Haden's voice sounded low and thick.

Without thinking, she licked her lips wanting to savor the last remnant of the kiss. She stood and watched Haden hurry down the hallway.

Alone, panic seized her.

What in the world just happened? She knew better than to get involved with her boss, and besides, there was Henry. He needed her.

But Haden had reminded her of what she had lost. She couldn't afford the hurt she knew would come. Everyone left.

Still dazed, she plopped into her chair and vowed that whatever this was, wouldn't ever happen again.

Then she remembered she'd agreed to go with him to his mom's house. She groaned inwardly. How could she avoid a guy who kissed like that and loved his mother?

Doomed.

Chapter Thirteen

Claire pulled up next to the curb not far from Betty Sawyer's mailbox. She wasn't sure she was ready for this, dinner with her fake boyfriend's family, but she hoped today would be the end of it. At least, that's what she told herself.

She grabbed her purse and Henry's back pack, which spilled over with all his necessary possessions. He couldn't be persuaded to leave the iPad nor his cape at home, though Claire had tried.

Stepping out of her car, she said, "Now, remember Henry, I expect you to use all your nice manners." She helped Henry on with his back pack.

"Are there bad ones, Mommy?" Henry asked as she reached for his hand.

"Bad what?" She asked.

"Manners. Are there bad manners? You said to use my nice ones, so are there bad ones?"

Claire drew in a deep breath. Henry had reached the age where every request was met with a question. "No, Henry. I meant be nice to everyone."

The petunias which lined the walkway to Betty's front porch stood straight as they reached for the warmth of the bright afternoon sun. The varying colors added a splash of whimsy to the otherwise green lawn. The hanging plants swaying in the light breeze of the April day gave motion to the unseen stirring all around them.

Reaching the porch, Claire rang the doorbell and waited. It wasn't long before the wood door swung open to reveal Betty Sawyer standing in her foyer wearing her Sunday dress covered with a red kiss-the-cook apron. She had donned her black and white zebra patterned slippers. "Oh! Come in, Come in. Haden isn't here yet. He ran home to change clothes."

"Oops, sorry. He told me any time after 12:30."

"Goodness, you're fine." Spotting Henry behind Claire, she said, "I found my old basket of wooden blocks along with some plastic animals and a car or two, Henry. I hope you like to build castles."

Henry peeked around his mother. "I like to draw them."

"Well, I've got a couple of pads of paper and some crayons on the bookshelf in the office if you want to go look for them."

"Cool." Henry pulled the screen door open and dashed into the house, dropping his backpack. The door sprung shut with a bang, causing Claire to flinch.

"It's the room with the big desk. Yes, right there." Claire and Betty watched Henry make his way around the staircase to the room opposite the living room.

"Henry," called Claire who was still standing on the porch. When Betty turned around, she radiated joy.

As Betty pushed the screen door open for her to enter, she said, "Claire, I am so glad you and Henry could join us today. It's done my heart a world of good to know Haden is moving on with his life. I was so afraid with Sarah being in town he might get tripped up." Betty grabbed Claire's arm and squeezed.

"Oh, I'm glad to be here, and thank you for the invitation on the phone yesterday."

"My pleasure. I didn't know if Haden had mentioned our family dinners or if it was too soon. How long have y'all been dating?" Betty took Claire's purse and hung it on one of the hooks, running along the wall beside the stair case. "Come with me into the kitchen."

Claire looked into the office as they passed. Henry laid on the floor in front of a love seat with pieces of paper spread all over the rug, talking to himself.

"We've been involved for a couple of weeks now." Claire figured this was as close to the truth as she could get.

Adele entered through the back door, using her elbow to close it since both of her hands were full. "Hello, hello. I've brought dessert, chocolate pie. Two to be exact."

"Here, let me help you with those." Jed offered and reached for them.

"Not on your life. Do I look like I was born yesterday?" She scooted past him, not letting him touch the pies.

"Oooh, maybe, we should eat dessert first," said Betty, lifting the foil off one of the pies. She wiggled her eyebrows and licked her lips, making a show of it.

Claire giggled at the antics. "It looks delicious."

"What looks delicious?" asked Haden who had somehow entered the room without Claire hearing him.

When she turned around, she found him standing a few steps away with Henry by his side. "I stopped to see what Henry was doing." He explained.

"What are those?" asked Henry as he ran towards the counter. Haden followed and lifted him from behind so he could see. It was such a natural act it caught Claire by surprise.

"What'd ya think Henry. Fit to eat?" asked Haden.

"Oh yeah," answer Henry as he stuck his finger in for a lick.

"Henry," Claire chided, but it was too late; her son was making himself at home.

Jed leaned on the counter and asked, "Can I have a finger full too?"

"Sure," answered Henry, but Claire shot her son a disapproving glance.

Betty swatted Jed's hand away as he tried to dip his finger into the whip cream topping.

"Let's leave the rest for after dinner," said Haden as Henry twisted in his arms to face him.

"Alright, if I have to."

"We'll make sure you get a piece." Jed said, placing the foil back over the pie with both Adele and Betty watching him like a hawk.

Adele leaned in towards Henry, who looked right at home in Haden's grasp. "I'll make sure you do."

A lump formed in Claire's throat. She swallowed hard trying to get it to relinquish its hold, but it didn't budge. In her mind, she framed this moment. Haden holding Henry; the older women fussing over their boys, and she labeled it family.

∞

After dinner, Claire followed Haden into the garden. She welcomed the relief from the afternoon of questions. Dinner had been delicious, but the inquisition which had gone hand in hand with the meal had left her with an upset stomach. She hated lying to Haden's family, and with each half-truth and side step, the knot in her stomach had grown.

The gentle warm breeze and the quiet of the garden worked to sooth away the tension.

As they walked along the garden path, Haden pointed out the various rows of beans, squash, and tomatoes as she followed close behind him.

The garden contained rows of small tender plants whose leaves still clung to crumbs of dirt. Claire noticed off to the left one lone mound of tiny new shoots.

"What's that?" she asked Haden who was straightening a tomato cage.

"That would be the annual mound of zucchini."

"Why just one mound? Everything else is laid out in full rows."

"Because no one eats zucchini." Haden sidled up beside her.

"Then why bother growing any at all?" Claire turned and discovered she was close enough to Haden to take his hand, but she fought the impulse by putting her hands into her jean pockets.

"Because we all love zucchini bread. As kids, Kyle, Jed, and I labeled it Houdini bread because once cooked, the bread vanishes. It's like magic."

"Cute." She said as her eyes held his. "This is a sweet little garden." Claire walked down the path between the row of tomatoes and beans. "I've always wanted to garden, but I don't have the time with Henry and all."

"How is Henry doing? I mean he seems so full of energy."

"He's having a good day." They had walked along the path to the edge of the garden where an old oak tree stood to the side, casting its shade over a wrought iron bench. The iron work resembled intricate lace.

"Henry's a good kid. You've done a great job with him."

Haden sat and patted the seat next to him. The fit was tight, so their legs touched as a matter of proximity. Claire's heart fluttered. She didn't like how her body reacted when he was close.

"Henry has transfusions of Immunoglobulin."

"That's a mouthful." Haden lifted his arm, draping it across the back of the bench.

Claire wiggled not sure how to sit to avoid physical contact with this man sitting next her, wearing the scent of musk. It hung on him like a loose shirt and teased her the same. "Yeah, but it's a game changer. He gets them about every four weeks and will for the next few months. We're hoping it's the push he needs to put his Juvenile Dermatomyositis into remission and allow him to grow."

"You mentioned that before. Is that part of it? The growth thing."

"It's a side effect of one of the treatments. This disease can cause a number of issues. Anything from a low-grade fever to digestive problems to calcium lumps forming under the skin, rashes. The most noticeable affect is the muscle weakness." Claire leaned back against the bench, worn out from the thought of what it meant.

"Explain to me what this disease is…exactly." Haden reached out and took her hand. Claire let him.

"Well, it's an autoimmune disease where the body is confused and attacks its own cells and tissues. This causes the patient…"

"Henry." Supplied Haden.

"Henry, a lot of pain."

"I see," said Haden, pulling Claire into his arms. Claire soaked in the warmth of his body. The comfort and support his strong arms lent. "Henry will be all right though, won't he? The doctors know what to do, and Henry will learn to cope with it."

Claire tensed. She always dreaded the question because the answer hurt her. Everyone wanted it to be sunshine and lollipops, but it wasn't. "There is no cure. There's only remission."

Claire waited for Haden to say something, to move away, to leave, but he didn't. Instead he let go of her hand and wrapped both arms around her, engulfing her as he whispered in her ear, "You are so brave."

∞

Haden let go with one arm long enough to retrieve his handkerchief from his back pocket.

The amount of water on the front of his shirt could be compared to puddles after a spring shower.

Claire hiccupped. "I don't know what came over me." She lifted her head from his shoulder to wipe her eyes with the handkerchief. "Sorry about your shirt."

"What, this old thing."

Claire smiled, causing her eyes to glisten. Haden's breath caught at the sight of the disheveled woman. Her hair tossed about by the wind; mascara streaked around her eyes due to the weeping. Her cheeks red, stained with tears, but he had never seen a lovelier creature in all his life than the woman who sat beside him. The openness of her heart made her beautiful.

Without thought, he leaned in to kiss her. The act came as natural to him as the sprouting of the plant came to the seed, but she turned.

"What?" He asked as he leaned his forehead against hers.

"We can't do this. It confuses me."

"What do you mean?" Haden leaned back giving Claire some space.

She pulled away and stood. "For one thing, you're my boss." She began to pace. "And for another, this is all made up. What happens when we tell everyone it's a lie? And what about Henry?" Claire stopped. "I have to think of Henry."

Haden stood, catching Claire's hands in his. "It's a kiss, Claire, and so far, it's been one. Can't we keep it low key and see where this takes us?"

"Low key. Haven't you been listening? I don't even think those words are in my vocabulary." Claire pulled her hands away and walked to the path that led through the garden. Stopping, she said, "My life, Haden, is anything but low key. If you can't handle the pressure, I suggest you get out of the kitchen."

"What does that even mean, Claire?" Haden sat back down on the hard metal bench with a thud. "And I think it's supposed to be if you can't stand the HEAT, get out of the kitchen."

Claire looked back over her shoulder at him but didn't slow her march to the back porch and the haven of the house.

"I think there was too much heat, there Cuz," said Kyle appearing with Daisey, his girlfriend, from behind the oak tree.

"You've got to be kidding me. Where on earth did you come from?" Haden leaned back on the bench and crossed his feet at the ankles, laying his arms across his middle.

"The tree, Cuz."

Daisey laughed at Kyle.

"Look, I'd appreciate it if you two could keep this to yourselves."

"What? The part about the relationship being fake, cause I already knew about that," Kyle looked at Daisey and winked. "Or the part where it got hot in the kitchen?" Kyle wiggled his eyebrows as his grin engulfed his face.

"Don't make me show you who's who. Just keep it all to yourself. Claire has enough to worry about without having to keep an eye on you."

"We won't tell," said Daisey. "I think it's so romantic the way you said she was brave and all."

Haden jumped up. "How long were you two eavesdropping?"

"Hold your horses there. We were here first. Daisey and I often retire to the oak tree after Sunday dinner. It's not my fault you didn't know we were here."

"It's true." Daisey's complexion redden as she leaned into Kyle who placed his arm around her. "This ole oak tree is one of our favorite places."

"Yes, it is." He said as he squeezed her closer. His eyes shining. "Now, if you'll excuse us, we'll get back to our Sunday resting."

Chapter Fourteen

Claire yanked her purse off the hook in the hall. Digging out her powder case, she used its small mirror to wipe the mascara from under her eyes. She licked the tissue she had found and dabbed at the smears punctuating the puffiness.

After applying a coat of powder to hide the redness, she went in search of Henry. She'd get Henry, pack his things, and leave.

But, Claire found Betty and Henry asleep in the office. Betty had stretched out on the loveseat while Henry had curled up in the chair, still holding one of the pictures he had colored. His ragged cape pulled over him.

Claire decided not to wake him. No matter how irritated she was with Haden, nor how much she wanted to leave the situation, Henry needed his sleep. She found a throw hanging over the back of the chair and laid it over him. As she left, she checked to make sure she hadn't disturbed Betty.

Not sure what to do with herself and unwilling to spend any more time with Haden, Claire returned to the kitchen and hunted for the plastic wrap. One by one, she covered the bowls of food sitting on the kitchen island. She heard Adele come through the doorway talking to someone. Glancing up, she found Sarah standing in front of her. Great.

"You shouldn't be doing that, girl. You're our guest." Adele walked over to snatch the plastic wrap dispenser out of her hand, but Claire moved too fast.

"Now, don't look a gift horse in the mouth. If we can eat, we can do our share of the clean-up. Besides, I'd do a thousand chores if I can have a second piece of your chocolate pie."

"Sold." Adele turned and gestured towards Sarah who moved closer to the island. "You've met Sarah, right?"

"Yes," answered Sarah before Claire could respond. "We met at the hospital the other day."

"Good to see you again." Claire wondered if her nose would grow with all these white lies she was telling.

"I stopped by to chat with Betty, but she's asleep in there," leaning closer to Adele and Claire, she said, "and I'd hate to wake her."

"Of course," said Claire.

"But I do think I'll say hello to Haden, if that's alright." Claire noted the twinkle of mischief in the woman's eyes.

"Of course, he's out in the back yard beyond the garden just take the path. It'll lead you right to him."

"You forget. I know the way." Sarah flashed Claire a coy smile and headed for the back door with her three-inch heels clicking all the way. Claire balled up her fist, fighting the urge to throw the bowl of macaroni and cheese at her.

Once the door closed, Adele said, "Don't let her get to you. The minute she heard you and Haden were an item she took it as a personal challenge to get him back."

"Why? Isn't she the one who left?"

"Because she's competitive. That was part of the trouble between her and Haden. She's all about the career and getting ahead. He wants something different, longer lasting."

"Well, it appears she's reconsidered." Claire frowned, not liking the sour feeling she had.

Adele came around the island and took her by her shoulders. "You need to decide. Do you want Haden, or don't you? Because if you don't, you need to let him have a chance with Sarah."

"What's there to decide. You know there is no us to decide about. It's all a lie."

"Are you sure?"

"What do you mean? Of course, I'm sure. I was standing right there when he told his mom."

"Are you sure it's a lie? Could there be some thread of truth mixed in?" Adele lowered her arms and released Claire. "Look I don't think there's a snowball's chance in July Haden is interested in Sarah. But you've got to decide if perhaps the lie and the truth aren't so far apart anymore."

"I don't know. I'm confused." Claire hated how she kept repeating herself. Why was she so confused? That kiss. He should never have kissed her. But, her mind wondered back to the warmth, the tenderness the kiss had held. A sigh escaped.

"I know you're confused. All you wanted was a job and now, you've been dragged into a drama you hadn't bargained for. So, here's my unsolicited advice. Clear everything else away, even Henry."

Claire groaned, shaking her head. "Can't be done. He's been my focus for so long. I've got to consider him."

"Clear everything away." Adele continued, "And ask yourself is

Haden the kind of man you want in your life?"

∞

Haden watched Sarah come out of the back door. He braced himself.

"Hey, I thought you were out in the garden. At least that's what your girlfriend told me."

The word girlfriend triggered a reaction in him he hadn't expected. It was easy to think of Claire as the girlfriend type, and even easier to think of her as his. It was too bad she was set on keeping all men at bay. She should come with a "no vacancy" sign over her heart.

"Yeah, that's where she left me earlier." Haden leaned forward, placing his forearms on his legs. He didn't want to talk about Claire with Sarah. "What brings you by today?"

"I thought I'd come visit Betty for a minute, but I found her and some little boy asleep in the office. I didn't want to wake them."

"Thanks. She needs all the rest she can get. She won't admit it, but she's slowed down a good bit. This cancer is taking its toll. I'll be glad when the procedure is behind us, and we can move on to the healing part."

"I am sorry you and your family's going through this," she said, placing her hand on his shoulder.

He hung his head. "It's something we hadn't counted on, but who does, right. To tell you the truth, when she first told us, it scared me silly. You know how I was after losing Dad. I couldn't imagine if Mom was to go."

Sarah sat beside him, stretching her arm across his back. "Haden, if there's anything I can do, you know all you have to do is ask."

Haden straightened, forcing Sarah to remove her arm. "It's okay. Between Aunt Adele, Jed, and Kyle, we've pretty much got everything covered."

"Sure, and I bet Claire's a big help."

"Claire has her own things she's dealing with. Her son has medical issues."

"Oh, is that the little boy?" Sarah stood and moved away. Haden wondered if she still felt the same as she did a year ago.

"Yeah, he's great. Mom's enjoyed having him around today."

"I'm sure she has." Sarah looked down at her designer shoes. "And what about you? Do you enjoy having him around?"

Haden tensed. "Let's leave that topic alone. We covered it before you left, and we don't need to rehash it now." His tone hardened. "Why are you here, Sarah? What do you expect to find?"

"I'd hoped for a warm welcome home." She let go of the swing's chain and crossed her arms. "But for now, I'll settle for a date to the Businessman's ball. I heard from Carol White you're not taking anyone."

"How nice of her to help with my dating situation." Haden leaned back in the swing wandering who he needed to thank for Sarah's sudden interest, Carol White or his Aunt Adele.

"Cute, Haden.

"Look, it wouldn't be a real date. The thing is I can't go unless I go as someone's plus one. The firm didn't put me on the attending list since they weren't expecting me until sometime in late May." She walked over and nudged Haden's knee with hers. "Come on, what'd ya say? Could you help out an old friend? Please?"

∞

The hot water flowed over the pile of dirty dishes causing bubbles from the soap to float up. Claire plunged her hands beneath the suds and hunted for the sponge. She kept looking at the time on the microwave. She told herself it was because she didn't want Henry to sleep too long or he wouldn't sleep later tonight.

However, as the minutes passed, she couldn't stop herself from peeking out the kitchen window over the sink to get a glimpse of Haden and Sarah. She scanned the back area by the oak tree but didn't see them. But as she began to pull away from the window, she heard a low murmur. Tilting her head to the left, she discovered them sitting on the back porch, a few feet from her.

What she wouldn't give to be able to make out their words.

She saw Sarah standing at an angle, and Haden sitting on the swing with his hands clasped together leaning his forearms on his knees.

Claire strained to get a better look, pressing her abdomen against the counter.

All she could see were the two of them talking, but it looked like a pleasant conversation from her view point.

Claire pulled away from the window unwilling to watch the two any longer. As she scrubbed the residue from the pot, she muttered, "Why bother with this charade? I thought you didn't want anything to do with Sarah."

In her irritation, Claire slammed the pot down into the empty side of the sink and pushed the curtain back. This time she saw Haden and Sarah sitting side-by-side. Sarah sat so close her leg touched his. She reached out and placed her arm around his shoulders. "What a rat!"

"Who are you talking to dear?" asked Betty.

Claire jumped. "No one." She pushed away from the counter, releasing the curtain. In her hurry, she knocked the scrubber off the edge of the sink into the soapy water. The splash drenched the front of her shirt.

"You're too young to start talking to yourself. Save that for later."

Claire pulled the dish towel from the hanger beside the window and folded the tail of her shirt into it.

"There you are," said Adele as she joined them in the kitchen. "Anyone up for a cup of coffee?"

"Yes, ma'am and a second piece of pie?" asked Betty.

"I owe Claire one for doing the dishes. But I think there's enough for three more slices."

"Me too?" asked Henry, rubbing his eyes.

Squatting to his level, Betty answered, "for you Henry, we'll make sure there's four."

"I like chocolate pie." Henry moved to the table and slid into a chair, resting his head on his arms. Adele got down four small plates from the china cabinet and placed them on the kitchen island.

Betty took the pie server and cut apart the last bit into four sections. Placing the slices on the plates, she carried two to the table, and Claire followed with the other two.

The three older individuals waited for the coffee to brew, but Henry dove into his piece.

The coffee filled the room with a rich aroma. Adele balanced the three cups of coffee in her hands, and Betty brought over the cream and sugar.

"That must've been good. You inhaled it," said Claire. Henry ran his finger over the top of the plate, catching any last crumbs.

Henry nodded and licked his finger.

∞

The back door swung open, allowing the aroma of the coffee to escape. "Smells good in here. Is there enough for two more cups?" asked Haden as he and Sarah entered the kitchen.

"Sure is, sweetie." Betty answered, "The cream and sugar are over here, though."

Sarah walked over to the cabinets, going straight to the right one which housed the mugs.

A twinge of jealousy reared its head. Claire ignored it. "How was your visit?' she asked as Sarah click-clacked her way across the tile floor to the table.

"Very nice. I asked Haden if he was taking anyone to the Businessman's ball, and he said to check with you." Sarah looked between Haden and Claire. Haden turned to get his coffee.

Claire sputtered and coughed. Adele reached over and patted her on the back. "Ask me?" Claire rasped.

"Yes, he said Carol White must've had it wrong, or it was an oversight or something."

Claire shot Haden a look.

"That's right, honey. I figured either Carol read it wrong, or you forgot to mark the plus one square on the card."

"Mommy, aren't you going to eat your pie?" asked Henry.

"No, you can have it." Claire stood and walked over to Haden who was leaning his backside against the counter.

She wrapped her arms around his middle and squeezed hard. "Well, dear, if you remember, I had been concerned about who would watch Henry while we were out. So, I hadn't marked anything." Claire looked up at Haden as he rested his right arm around her.

"Oh, great, then you can be my date," said Sarah as she took Claire's seat at the table.

Claire squinted her eyes and set her jaw. "I was going to say I hadn't marked anything at the time."

"I take it you've thought about it and want to go, honey?" Claire watched Haden's brown eyes soften. They welcomed her into his world like his arms had welcomed her to his side.

"Yes, I do," answered Claire as Haden pulled her closer. The feel of his hand on her back and the gentle kiss he placed on the top of her head soaked into her like soft rain on dry ground.

"Good," he said. "Tomorrow, I'll call Carol and make sure she has you in her count."

For a moment, she stood by his side wrapped in his embrace, wanting the lie to be the truth. It made her think about what Adele had asked her.

"Well, I've got my answer," said Sarah, "I'd better go. Betty, Adele, it was good to see you." Sarah stood to leave. "I'm sure we'll run into each other again now that I'm staying in that cute little apartment above the flower shop. You know the one, Haden. You and Jed did the renovations on it."

"Yeah, I know the one. Is the shop still empty?"

"Yeah, the land lord is letting me lease on a month by month bases while I look for a house."

"Month by month sounds good," said Claire. She didn't mean it to sound so biting, but the comment brought the strained conversation to a screeching halt.

"Let me walk you out," offered Adele.

As the kitchen cleared, Betty started to drag a chair over to the sink for Henry so he could help wash up the plates and coffee mugs. Haden cut her off before she got more than a few inches. "I'll do that. Just tell me where you want it."

Betty patted his hand as he took the chair from her. "By the sink please. Henry is going to help me wash the dishes."

"Oh yeah. Score. Can I play in the bubbles?" Henry struggled, trying to climb into the chair. Haden came behind him and gave him a little boost. "Thanks"

"No problem, sport."

Haden placed his mug into the soapy water with the others and grabbed Claire's hand. Claire followed as he led her to the office. "I wanted to thank you for saving my hide with Sarah."

"You know you didn't look like you needed saving while you were sitting knee to knee with her on the swing." Claire didn't mean to sound so harsh, but it hurt seeing him with her.

"What are you talking about?"

"I saw you two, out the window."

"You were spying on us?"

Claire looked down to avoid meeting his gaze.

"No. I was curious. That's all."

Haden took Claire by her shoulders. "For someone whose just curious, you sound a bit jealous to me."

Claire reddened. "You two looked so cozy. I'm surprised you minded going to the ball with her."

"To be clear, I do mind. I'd rather spend my evening with you."

"Great, now I'm a consolation prize." Claire crossed her arms. Haden threw his hands into the air.

"You are impossible." He ran his hand down his face. "Do you or do you not want to go with me to the ball?"

"I said I'd go; I'll go."

"But do you want to go?"

Henry lumbered into the room. "Mom, my arms hurt."

"Did you have fun helping Miss Betty?" Claire turned from Haden to Henry, thankful for the interruption.

"Yeah, but we both think we need another nap." Henry leaned up against her, hugging her leg.

"I think I better go," she said, reading the frustration in Haden's face.

"So, I'll contact Carol tomorrow?"

Claire heard the uncertainty in his voice. She started to gather Henry's belongings and stuff them into his backpack for the drive home. "Yes, do that." Then ashamed of her behavior she met his gaze. "And Haden, I do want to go."

Haden nodded but didn't reply.

"Mom will you carry me?" asked Henry as he flopped onto the loveseat.

"I'll get'cha sport." Haden lifted Henry over his shoulder like a sack of potatoes. "Comfy?"

Giggling, Henry said, "Y-e-e-s," as Haden did a light jog to the door, causing Henry to bounce.

Chapter Fifteen

The bell on the door jingled as Claire pushed her way through into the café. The Wednesday lunch crowd filled every booth, and the only seat available was at the counter. Claire hurried over and grabbed it.

Adele spied her and called out, "Your order'll be ready in a minute, honey. That was two burgers, a bacon cheeseburger for Haden, and three fries, right?"

"You got it." While she waited, Claire pulled her phone out to check her emails. She was expecting a confirmation email from the Chamber of Commerce about the Charity Ball, but it hadn't come yet.

Monday, Haden had contacted Carol White to let her know to add a plus one for him. Claire tried to play it down, but she couldn't shake the knots in her stomach.

The Charity Ball, however, wasn't the reason for her distress. It was Haden. The kiss, his dimples, the scent of his musk cologne, those accounted for the bulk of her mental tension. She had to fight to keep her mind on her work.

But what occupied her heart was the way he was with Henry, so natural. That's what bothered her. Sunday had given her a glimpse of what she and Henry were missing - family.

As Adele rounded the counter with an arm load of dirty dishes, she asked, "How's Henry? Did he enjoy himself Sunday?"

"He had a great time. He's never had a grandmother, and you two did a great job of spoiling him."

"Good. Betty and I love kids." Adele deposited the dirty dishes in the bus tub. "We can't wait to be grandmother's ourselves, but at the rate our boys are getting married, we may wind-up being cat ladies. Of course, there's nothing wrong with cats, but they're not kids." Adele shot a look down the counter to where Kyle, her son, sat.

Claire giggled. "I can't see you or Betty babying a bunch of cats."

Adele leaned in. "Me neither, but you have to have a plan B. So, what's Haden been up to?" She removed a couple of mugs from off the counter and deposited them into the bus tray, too.

"To be honest, he's been a little distant. Yesterday, he spent all day holed up in his office. This morning bright and early, he left to see Charlie Lee, the president of the Businessman's League. Said he had something he needed to discuss with him, but he never said what."

Adele waved off the comment. "Sounds like business to me. There are times you have to sit down and do the paperwork. Not me of course," she added, "but most business people. I hate paperwork. I have my accountant do the taxes, and Frank does inventory for me. That's why I keep him around."

Claire hoped Adele was right. Maybe Haden was busy. "Speaking of Frank, is my order ready?"

"Not yet. Frank's been a little slow today. I'm keeping my eye on him."

"I don't need your eye on me, Adele Sawyer." Frank called from the pick-up window as he placed another plate on the shelf. "It's my arthritis acting up. Nothing serious."

"I got it honey." Cherie hustled up to the window and grabbed the plate, placing it in front of Kyle. "Can I get you anything else, sweetie?"

"No, this looks good."

"Does Daisey know you've got another woman?" asked Claire.

"Oh, Daisey knows all about my other women, but she's not worried. Hey, I heard from Aunt Betty that you and Haden are going to the Businessman's Ball."

Claire sighed. "I agreed to go with him."

"Well, I would think so since you two are an item." Kyle winked at her.

Claire hated lies. It made it hard to remember who knew what. Jed and Adele knew it was a farce. To her knowledge, Kyle and Daisey and Betty didn't. She didn't know what Carol White knew, and at this point, she wasn't sure if she, herself, knew the truth.

Putting on a smile, she tried again. "We are planning to go if I can find a babysitter for Henry."

"No problem. Daisey and I can cover it."

"Aren't you two going to the ball?"

"No, it's not my speed. I let the old fogies handle those events."

"Wait a minute. Are you calling me an old fogy?" Claire swiveled her stool to get a better look at Kyle. His smile traveled up, becoming a sparkle in his eye.

"No, ma'am. I am not."

"Ma'am. You better watch it, buster."

"So, what about the babysitting? We'd be glad to. Daisey enjoyed playing with Henry Sunday. I know she'd be all in."

"When did she play with Henry?" asked Adele. "We barely saw her or you for that matter."

"We had time before dinner. She helped him color a T-rex. They added flames coming off its feet. Pretty awesome."

"I appreciate the offer but taking care of Henry involves a lot more than entertaining him. There's his medicine he takes before bed, and the exercises. Plus, it can be hard to get his full co-operation sometimes. I'd hate to put you and Daisey through that."

"Look, Daisey and I won't break Henry. I promise. You write down the instructions, and we'll follow them to the letter."

Claire scrutinized him for a minute. "You're sure the two of you can handle it?"

"Scouts honor," said Kyle, raising his left hand in a three-fingered salute.

Adele snorted. "Wrong hand." She leaned towards Claire. "He never did Scouts."

"Really, this is how it starts? What is it with Sawyer's and the truth?"

Adele cleared her throat and shook her head. Claire took her warning and quickly added, "There's another hitch."

"What would that be?" Adele set the bags of take-out, down on the counter in front of Claire and propped her hand on her ample hip.

"I don't have anything to wear. And I don't have any extra cash to splurge to get something either." Claire fished around in her wallet and pulled out the exact amount for the order.

"Why are you paying for lunch for the office? I could understand you paying for your own, but it looks like you're picking up the whole tab."

"It's no big deal. I've been paying for the lunches. Haden forgets, and I'm uncomfortable with asking him to reimburse me."

"You should use the petty cash," said Kyle in between bites of his meatloaf. "That's what it's for."

"I didn't know there was a petty cash fund."

"I bet Haden collected it from Doris before he hired you. He must've forgotten to replace it." Kyle shrugged. "I'm sure it was an oversight. You might want to mention it to him. I'm sure he'll want to reimburse you once he knows."

"I'll be sure to tell him, but it doesn't help me with my issue of nothing to wear to the event. Those few dollars won't be enough to buy the kind of dress I'll need."

"Well, I might have an answer for you Cinder-Claire," said Adele.

"What are you talking about? What's Cinder-Claire?"

"Think of me as your Fairy Godmother, and you're Cinderella. I'll take care of the outfit." Adele straightened and dug out a pen and pad from her apron pocket. "Write down your dress and shoe size. I'll be in charge of putting together your outfit."

"Adele, I can't let you do that. It's too much." Claire's imagination shifted into overdrive. What kind of dress could she expect?

"Enough, enough, Cinder-Claire. Your Fairy Godmother has spoken. It won't cost much of anything." Adele pushed the pad towards her. "Now, write it down and disappear in a puff of smoke, so I can get busy on making the magic happen."

Claire stared, holding the pen, unsure of what to do. Adele tapped the pad. "Write it down."

Claire shrugged and started writing. "I think you're the one who's supposed to disappear in a puff of smoke."

"Maybe, but in this version, I own the store and still have to put in a full day's work."

∞

The sun kissed Claire's cheeks as she made her way down the sidewalk, heading towards Sawyer Construction. She paused as she passed Maybell's, one of the four clothing boutiques in Miller Creek.

The dress in the window shimmered in the light. Silver sparkles ran down the right shoulder and across the midsection, continuing down the left side of the skirt. The crisscross of the bodice formed a nice waistline. The sky-blue hue of the dress she knew would accent her green eyes.

Ryan had loved her in blue. She stopped herself from going down that rabbit hole.

As she gazed at the dress, all she heard was Adele calling: Cinder-Claire, Cinder-Claire. Adele's talk of Cinderella had triggered her desire to feel pretty once more, to have a man think of her as beautiful.

The dress called to her.

What could it hurt?

So, disregarding the bags of food in her hand, she pushed open the door to the boutique. The rush of sweet smells caused a slight thrill to shoot through her. How long had it been since she treated herself to a shopping spree? From the feelings zinging through her, too long.

A blonde sales lady dressed in flowing fabrics approached her. "Can I help you, miss."

Miss? Much better than ma'am.

"Yes, I was admiring the blue dress in the window. You don't happen to have it in a size ten, do you?"

"We do. Follow me." The sales lady led Claire to the back of the store. "It's a magnificent piece. We got it in a few weeks ago." She pulled the dress from the rack and tried to hand it to Claire, but between the bags of food and her purse, her hands were full.

"Why don't you set your things on the counter, and I'll hang the dress in the second dressing room."

Claire looked at the bags. She knew the food was getting cold. So, what if Haden had to eat a cold burger. He'll get over it.

She hustled across the floor and put the items on the counter.

As she passed the mirror, hanging between the dressing room doors, she caught a glimpse of herself and stopped. Her brunette hair needed a cut. It hung limp in the ponytail that she had grown accustomed to wearing. She wore a brown plaid cotton button down with the Sawyer Construction logo on it and pair of old ragged jeans. On her feet, she sported a pair of Converse tennis shoes. The most stylish thing on her body.

What happened to me? Claire leaned in closer to the mirror, examining the hair that framed her face. Gray.

Feeling betrayed by her own image, she squared her shoulders and marched into the dressing room. As she fingered the fabric, a burst of glee exploded inside her.

The dress fit like a glove, a beautiful, exquisite, soft as silk glove.

"Do you need help with the zipper?" asked the sales lady.

"Yes, please." Claire opened the door and stepped out. The sales lady stared.

"Aw, honey, you look like something out of a fairy tale."

As she reached to zip the back, she added, "Of course, you'll need to do something with that hair." She must've heard what she said because she tried to clarify. "I mean how you have it now is fine for every day, but with a dress like this one, you'd want to do something extra special."

Claire marveled at the imagine before her. The simple change of clothes made a huge difference. The blue of the dress drew the green of her eyes out to where they popped. The silver sparkles added a glow to her natural skin tone.

The sales lady was correct, though. The hair needed help. Claire reached up and wrapped the ponytail into a bun. Holding it, she twirled in front of the mirror looking from the front to the back several times.

"Stunning," came a male voice that held a deep tremor.

Claire whirled around to find Haden leaning against the counter, holding the bags of food.

"What are you doing here?" She released her hair, allowing herself to transform back into the everyday Claire.

"I came to rescue my food. When Kyle told me, you had left while he was still eating, I thought you might have gotten lost. I see it was something more important." Haden's dimples emerged one at a time as his smile grew. His teasing eased her worry from earlier.

"What a lovely dress." Haden straightened and crossed the floor towards her, "and if I might be allowed to say so, it's lovely on you." Haden was now standing in front of her. He reached up and ran his hand down her cheek. "It makes you sparkle, especially your eyes."

Claire couldn't help herself. She melted into his touch. The thought of his kiss swept through her mind, and she tilted her chin and lifted her head inviting him to repeat it.

∞

Watching Claire as she inspected herself in the mirror had seemed like an invasion of her privacy, but Haden couldn't turn away.

As he removed his hand from her cheek, he had the urge to lean forward and test the sweetness of her lips. Her eyes beckoned to him. Her upturned head, the slight tilt of her chin, they all called to him, but her words from Sunday rang in his ears. He didn't want to confuse her.

That thought acted like a bucket of cold water on his desire. He stepped back. "I've got to go. I'm supposed to meet Ted Henderson at his house to check the delivery." Handing her the bag with her lunch in it, he turned on his heels and hustled for the door. "Thanks for picking up food," he called over his shoulder.

Stopping at the door, he added, "Kyle mentioned you've been paying for the lunches." He pointed to the bag he held in his hand. "I'll be sure to put the petty cash box back in your desk. I forgot after we hired you. Let me know how much Sawyer Construction owes you, and I'll be sure to cut you a check." Haden stood staring for a moment, before pushing the door open with his backside and stepping out into the warm April afternoon.

"Stupid." He muttered as he stomped towards the trailer.

He kicked the gravel in the parking lot, sending it skittering in different directions. "Stupid, stupid, stupid. I should've kissed her."

Haden threw the bag into his pick-up truck and cranked the engine to a roar. He opened the bag with one hand and pulled out the cold bacon cheeseburger. Even cold, the burger would help. As he drove, he replayed the scene in his Mom's garden.

Claire had been a mess after crying; yet, all he saw was the beauty of a brave woman. Now, he'd seen her sparkling like diamonds which left him wanting more than she was willing to give, her heart.

Shaking his head, he groaned. The word "Stupid," rolled off his tongue without thinking. "Confused," joined it.

Confused. She picked the right word.

Between the mixed signals she was giving him, and trying to keep straight who knew what, confused fit. Shoot, he lived there.

"Great, I'm stupid and confused." Haden tore into the Henderson's driveway, bringing the pick-up to an abrupt halt.

He jumped out and grabbed his clipboard from off the front seat. Kicking the door, it slammed with a thud.

"Hey, there Haden. Something chasing you?" asked Wayne, one of his foremen.

"Yeah, but there's nothing I can do about it right now." Haden walked over to the materials scattered in a make shift pile and began working.

After sorting through half of it, Haden took a break. In the hour he'd been there, he'd managed to work off some of his frustration. Then he spotted Sarah Dempsey standing in the yard talking with Wayne. Just what he needed.

Haden stalked over to see what she wanted.

"How can I help you?" Haden addressed Sarah, but it was Wayne who answered.

"She wanted to drop off the specs for the remodel of the hospital. Her architect firm is doing the job."

"Yeah, I know," said Haden, cutting his eyes toward Wayne. "Why don't you let Sarah, here, explain."

Holding his hands up in surrender, Wayne said, "Okay, you're the boss."

As he stepped away, Haden handed him the clipboard. "Go finish up."

Wayne took it. "Sure thing."

"Now, what's going on?" Haden asked.

"The firm thought you'd like an opportunity to bid on the remodel job at the hospital. Your name kept coming up; you have a stellar reputation. So, I wanted to hand deliver the specs. That's all." Sarah held out the paperwork to him. Her three-inch heel sunk into the grass as they talked.

Haden's hands stayed in his pockets. "I don't mean to sound ungrateful…"

"But you're going to anyway, right?"

Haden met her hard stare. "Yeah, I am. I don't see how it can be good for either of us to put ourselves in the situation where we'll have to work together on a regular basis. I just don't want people to get the wrong idea."

"You mean you don't want your girlfriend slash secretary to get the wrong idea." Sarah shifted her weight from one hip to the other and crossed her arms. A sign Haden recognized as irritation. She didn't take no, well. "Is that your final decision? You're going to let your love life dictate your professional life."

"You betcha." Haden crossed his arms and planted his feet.

Chapter Sixteen

Claire pulled into the Henderson driveway, maneuvering around the other vehicles parked hodge-podge all over the yard. Her Ford rambled to a halt right behind Haden's truck.

She grabbed the work order from the passenger seat. She wanted to wring someone's neck. How they missed getting all the necessary signatures was beyond her. "Men," she mumbled as Wayne, the foreman, passed her.

"Hey Wayne, where's Haden? I need to get his signature."

Wayne stopped and back tracked.

"I wouldn't bother him if I were you. He's in a mood." Wayne tucked the clipboard under his arm.

"It doesn't matter. I need to see him. I don't think it can wait."

"Suit yourself." Wayne pointed towards the right of a clump of pine trees. "He's over there talking to Sarah Dempsey about bidding on the hospital job."

"Oh." Claire hugged the paperwork to her when she spotted them.

Haden stood tall, feet planted with his arms crossed over his chest. He looked like a tower. The hard look on his face spoke volumes. "He does look…firm."

Wayne chuckled. "That's a good way to describe him. Firm. When she showed up, he firmly gave me the clipboard and firmly dismissed me."

"Sarah does have that effect on him."

"Yes, I imagine she does, but I thought that was all water under the bridge. Rumor has it he's got a new lady friend."

Claire's cheeks colored. "I've heard that rumor too."

Wayne raised his brows, "You're not the friend, are you?"

"I think I am."

"Me and my big mouth." Wayne shook his head and walked off.

Claire moved towards Haden who had part of his back to her. Claire caught Sarah's attention first, and with cat like prowess, she sidled up beside Haden, putting her hand in the crook of his elbow.

The sour look on Haden's face told Claire all she needed to know.

"Hi there, you two," said Claire as she grabbed a hold of his other elbow and bent him towards her, placing a quick peck on his cheek.

Two can play at this game, Missy.

Sarah didn't relinquish her hold on him.

"Where did you come from?" Confusion colored Haden's face.

"Originally or just now?" Claire pasted a smile on her face.

"She's a gem. I can see why you love working with her. I bet she keeps everyone in stitches." Sarah turned to face Haden as best as she could with her heels sunk in the ground. "Now, I want you to promise me you'll think about my little proposition." Here, she winked.

Claire's jaw tightened. How dare she make business sound like monkey-business. If Wayne hadn't told her what was going on, Sarah could've caused her and Haden a lot of trouble.

"I've given you my answer. I don't have to think about it. Sawyer Construction won't be bidding on the job."

Sarah dropped her hand. "Fine, I'll let my firm know your decision. But personally, I think you're acting rather childish. I'm sure Claire wouldn't mind if we worked together."

"To be honest, I think it would be terrible."

"Why? We've worked well together in the past."

"That's before you broke his heart."

"Claire, stop." Haden placed his hand over hers and squeezed.

"You don't deserve to waltz back into his life demanding his time. Whether he has a girlfriend or not." Claire pulled her hand away from Haden's and took a step closer to Sarah.

"You need to stay out of this." Haden stepped in front of her.

"No, I don't. I might not have signed up for this, but she has no right to hound you. Showing up at your mom's, traipsing out here where you're working. She hasn't given one thought to how this might affect you." Claire clenched her fists.

Sarah came around Haden. "I had every right to visit Betty. I've known the family a lot longer than you." Sarah's lips flattened into a thin line and her eyes became slits.

"I'm sorry. Can you excuse us for a minute?" Haden grabbed Claire by the arm and turned her towards her truck.

He whispered in her ear as they walked, "You are way out of line."

"I need to go, anyway," Sarah called. "I have work of my own to do. But I won't forget this. I'll think twice before I try to help you out again, since it bothers your little girlfriend here so much."

Claire jerked her arm out of Haden's grasp and bolted for Sarah. Sarah tried to move, but her three-inch heels refused to budge, trapping her where she stood.

Claire stopped inches from her face. "If I weren't a lady, I'd clobber you."

"I don't know what Haden finds so irresistible about you that he'd turn down a great opportunity like this."

"I don't think he finds me irresistible; I think he finds me reliable." Claire cringed. She knew she'd gone too far, but everything about the woman set her on edge.

Sarah's face blanched. "You might want to get your facts straight." Leaning over, she pulled her feet from her shoes, yanked them out of the ground, and stormed to her car.

"I can't believe you did that."

Claire turned, catching her first glimpse of Haden. She had been so focused on Sarah, Haden had slipped into the background. Now, he stood front and center.

Firm.

"You are something else." His voice rose.

"Don't yell at me. I did you a favor." Claire stepped forward coming within reach of Haden.

"A favor? How do you figure?" His brows furrowed as he propped his fists on his hips.

"She won't be nosing around you anymore. I've marked my territory."

"What are you a Labrador Retriever? I'm not territory."

"How dare you! You ungrateful, man."

"Ungrateful? You just cost me a good connection to other jobs because you made assumptions like everyone else in this town. You can't go around insulting people we depend on for our livelihood."

"Why do I even bother?" Claire threw her hands up in disgust, papers and all. "I'm out of here." She did an about face and marched to her truck, forgetting about the needed signature. She heard Haden behind her before he stepped in her way. He stood so close she could feel the heat from his breath.

"Stop, you can't go like this." His volume decibels lower than it had been.

"Why not?" Claire bent her head back so she could see his face.

"Cause everyone is staring. I don't want it to get around town we've been fighting. It'll make Mom worry, and it'll give Sarah a reason to come back around."

"Oh, so my standing up for you helped? Is that what you're saying?"

Haden grimaced and rolled his eyes. "Maybe, now kiss me so I can get back to work."

"I'm not kissing you." Claire hugged the paperwork to her chest and stood tall.

"Yes, you are," said Haden bending near her ear. "If you can kiss me hello, you can kiss me good-bye."

Claire cut her eyes from side to side. She hated to admit it, but he was right they had drawn a crowd. Everyone watched to see the outcome.

She faced him, tip-toed, and placed a simple kiss on his lips.

"It needs to be believable." Haden reached down and placed his hand on the nape of her neck. The warmth of his hand sent a surge of energy through her body.

He led her mouth to his. His lips brushed softly over hers, but it didn't satisfy her. She needed more.

She ran her hand up his chest to his shoulder and brushed her lips against his again with more hunger. He gathered her closer, wrapping his left arm around her waist.

She melted into him. He deepened the kiss.

When Haden pulled back, he leaned his forehead to hers. As she caught her breath, Haden whispered, "That should do the trick."

∞

That evening after work, Adele headed to Betty's house with the items she had purchased on her lunch hour, which had turned into two. She had enjoyed the thrill of being the Fairy Godmother. Going to the different stores, looking for just the right pair of heels to match the dress, and making Claire a hair appointment with her girl, Kelli.

Now as she bustled towards Betty's back door with her treasures, her heart filled with excitement.

She found her sister-in-law upstairs in her bed resting. Adele thought Betty's bedroom reflected her personality. Cheery yellow sunflowers dominated the décor. They peppered the curtains, the throw at the end of the bed and the chair that sat in the corner of the room.

Adele stood near the closet at the side of the bed and held up the blue dress for Betty to see.

"It's perfect. Is it her size?"

"Yes, I had her write down all her sizes, dress, shoes, and personal items. In case I needed to go shop for a dress. Thank goodness, Wendy's a ten, too."

Betty leaned forward on the bed and touched the dress. "It sparkles.

She'll be the belle of the ball."

Adele glowed with pride. "Wait till you see the shoes." She draped the dress across the pillows piled next to Betty on the bed and fished the shoe box out of the Sole Parade bag. It had taken Adele an hour to decide between two pairs. Now, she was confident she'd made the right choice.

"Oooh," cried Betty as Adele lifted the lid. "These will put Cinderella's glass slippers to shame."

Adele giggled. It had been awhile since she'd enjoyed shopping as much as she had today.

"Wait till you see the lacey slip and under garments I got to go with it."

"You've thought of everything." Betty blushed a gentle pink. "You don't think Claire will get the wrong idea. Think we are assuming more of the relationship than we are?" Betty's eyes grew wide.

"Oh, no. Claire's a woman of the twenty-first century. She'll know we want her to be comfortable. Look her best." Adele winked. "Besides, I don't even know if the young women of today know about what goes with what. I mean from what some of the young ladies' wear at Super-mart. You'd think the whole concept of seasons has gone out the window. I remember when you'd be shunned if you wore white after Labor Day."

"Yes." Betty leaned back on her pillow, pulling the throw to her waist. "I remember when Otis made fun of me for tearing the house apart one Sunday, looking for my dark pumps. He stood in the doorway holding a pair of white open-toed heels saying 'what's wrong with these? You wore them last week.' He didn't understand fashion at all." A sweet smile played on Betty's lips.

"I also picked up a purse." Adele produced it from the depths of the bag.

Betty rolled to her side to look at it. Adele perched it next to the shoe box. "Do you think it matches?"

"Perfect. Claire's lucky to have such an attentive fairy godmother." Betty raised up on her elbow. "You know, I'm not sure what the weather is going to be like Friday. Do you think she'll need a wrap?'

"It'd probably be best for her to take one; don't you think?"

"Definitely, I have a silver one with fringe. It might do the trick," said Betty.

"Umm, on second thought, maybe we should send her off without one. You know give Haden the chance to prove chivalry isn't dead by offering her his jacket."

"You, sly old dog. I see why you're the pro." Betty laid back against the pillows and burrowed down into the top one. She sighed as she closed her eyes.

"I hope Haden can see himself beyond now. If he can get a vision of what life with someone like Claire would be like, I think he'd understand the better truth."

"What better truth?" Adele gathered the items and placed them back in the bag, making room for Betty to stretch out. She opened the closet and turned her back to Betty while she worked.

"That life is always better when we are loving others. I think Haden has forgotten what love can do for you. Sarah took it from him, but…" Betty mumbled something, then silence filled the room.

Adele turned from the closet to find Betty with her eyes closed.

Her breath creating a light snore.

Worry washed over Adele as she stood watching her friend. She looked so delicate, so fragile. The cancer had caused her to lose weight, and she knew the chemo and radiation after the surgery would only add to the problem.

How she wished the surgery were over. She needed to know what they were dealing with. She needed to know Betty was going to be all right.

Chapter Seventeen

Haden tossed and turned in bed. He inhaled and Claire's lavender scent overwhelmed him. Her perfume lingered on his shirt, lying on the floor by his closet.

The kiss from yesterday had left him reeling. They seemed to have some sort of weird courting ritual. First, they fought; then they kissed. Both activities were done with equal amounts of passion. Too bad they weren't even dating.

Haden turned over onto his side. Sleep evaded him. He knew a long full day lay ahead, which included the Businessman's Annual Charity Ball, but every time he closed his eyes, Claire filled his mind, with her hair up in a ponytail, wearing that brown plaid shirt. If she thought she fit in better with the crew by wearing it, she had another thought coming. She was curvier than any construction worker he'd ever seen.

"Great," he muttered as he rolled to his back to check the time. One o'clock.

He punched the pillow, fluffing it anew. He turned his back on the clock.

Now, Sarah was a different problem. She didn't like to lose. From what Claire said about marking her territory, he didn't think she liked it much either.

Every time he saw Sarah now, he realized how wrong they would've been together. He knew after he discovered she didn't want children that the chasm was too great. Family rooted him, and he wanted one of his own.

Breaking off the engagement had been the right thing to do but letting everyone think Sarah had up and cut ties, well, it plagued him. Everyone had made the assumption she had ended things when she left two weeks before the wedding. From what Claire said today, even she had jumped to that conclusion.

He grinned at the thought of Claire standing up for him. Eyes blazing, fist clinched. Sarah with her heels stuck in the mud. He'd been relieved Claire hadn't pushed her over in it. There for a minute, he thought she might. He chuckled to himself and checked the clock.

Two a.m.

Haden exhaled to release his pent-up tension. With his eyes wide open, he could see Claire standing in front of the mirror at Maybelle's trying on the sparkling blue dress, her eyes dancing.

What was he thinking, dragging her into his situation with Sarah? So, what if his mother and Aunt were on an all-out campaign for grandchildren.

I was thinking, what a wonderful sense of humor she has, and how she blushes a soft pink, and what a great mom she is. I was thinking how much I wanted to get to know her. I was thinking how good her lips would taste –

"Shut up," Haden growled, slamming his eyes closed.

Sometime around five thirty, the alarm blared filling the room with the latest in country hits. As George Strait crooned about losing the girl, Haden reached over and lowered a hammer fist onto the device. George fell silent.

After showering, he stood in his closet half dressed with his blue jeans on and no shirt, wondering which tie would go with his dark brown suit.

"Don't do it," said Kyle, causing Haden to jump.

"I swear I'm getting pad locks for my doors."

Kyle laughed. "Got any coffee?"

"No, I haven't made any yet. I'm trying to figure out what to wear to the dinner tonight."

"That's why I'm here. My mom sent this over." Kyle walked back into the hall and reappeared carrying a plastic hanging bag.

"What is it?"

"I don't know. She said something about a Fairy Godmother. I believe it's a replacement for that antiquity." Kyle nodded toward the suit hanging on the hook of the closet door.

"I'll have you know it's my best suit."

"No, that was your best suit about ten years ago. Don't you have anything else? I mean you've been to this dinner before."

"Yeah, I've got a black suit I wear to most things, but I don't know. It's got snags, and the coat's missing a button."

"Whatever. All I know is it's time to retire that thing."

"This suit's gotten me plenty of dates; I'll have you know."

"Only out of pity, man. The suit goes."

Haden moved in front of it facing Kyle. "What if I don't want to give it up?" Haden crossed his arms over his bare chest.

Kyle stood taller, rolling his shoulders back to reach his full height. "My mom wants you to wear this suit." Kyle held the hanging bag up in his left hand and pointed with his right to Haden. "You'd be wise to do as she wishes."

"Oh, would I?" Haden cocked an eyebrow.

"How bout I show you the suit before you get all bent out of shape. I bet you'll like it. You want to make a good impression on Claire, don't you?" Kyle walked over to the bed and threw the garment bag across it.

"Yeah, I do, but it's been a long time since anyone bought clothes for me. I usually do that myself. Being an adult and all."

Kyle nodded. "I see your point, but man, that brown suit is not the ticket. Mom probably knew you'd be too busy to think about what to wear. Plus, I know Mom and Aunt Betty have a lot riding on this date tonight."

Haden walked over and watched as Kyle pulled a stylish navy-blue suit from the bag. He also saw a crisp white shirt on a hanger in the back with a tie looped around the hanger's neck. The swirls of blue in the tie's design reminded Haden of a dark stormy sky.

"Wow, I can't believe Aunt Adele did this. I'll have to be sure and thank her."

"Believe it. If she thinks it gets Aunt Betty closer to grandchildren, she's all in."

"I wonder how we could milk that?" Haden grinned and nudged Kyle with his elbow. Kyle handed over the suit.

"Mom told me to have you check the size. She'll need to know in case she has to exchange it before this evening."

Haden took the coat off the hanger and pulled it over his broad shoulders. The cut hugged his body, but he could move his arms well enough. The sleeves hit right along the wrists where they should. Picking up the pants, he looked for the tag with the size on it. He found it inside the waist band. "Yep, these'll do." He held the pants up against his jeans.

"Great. Now that I've got your wardrobe issue solved. I'm gonna go fix the coffee problem."

∞

Friday afternoon rolled past in a blur. First Claire looked for pantyhose. She went to three different stores before she found the right shade. They made the size charts impossible to read. Then she stopped by the drug store for some clear nail polish. A three o'clock hair appointment with Kelli had ended at half past five, getting her home minutes before she was to meet Adele.

Now, Claire looked at her reflection in the full-length mirror. Adele had brought over a hanging bag and a tote filled with shoes, a purse, and a silvery shawl and a few other unmentionables.

As far as Fairy Godmothers go, this one thought of everything. The act of putting on those unmentionables with spandex and elastic in them had been worthy of a spot on Funniest Home Videos. But everything else had fit less like the preverbal glove. Thank goodness.

Claire waited to open the hanging bag until last, not wanting to be disappointed with Adele's selection.

How had Adele known? She slipped the sky-blue dress over her hips and turned from side to side admiring the shimmer of the light as it hit the sparkles.

"You look like the princess in my book, Mommy," Henry said as he entered the room and peeked around the full, knee length skirt of the dress.

"Well, you and Baby are my handsome princes." Claire squatted so she could kiss Henry on the cheek.

"No, we're pirates." With that, Henry began to wield his imaginary sword throwing himself onto Claire's bed. His red cape twirled around him as he rolled to a stop on the pillows.

"Now, remember," said Claire as she stood. "Kyle and Daisey are going to sit with you tonight. So, you and Baby have to be on your best behavior. No, getting out of bed a bunch of times and don't let Baby get near the crack."

"Okay, Mommy. Will they give me a bedtime snack?" Henry sat on the bed, watching her put on her diamond studded earrings. His energy levels had been a little higher since the recent infusion.

"Yes, it's on the list."

"Will they read me a story?"

"Yes, that's on the list too," answered Claire as she sat on the side of the bed to put on her shoes.

"Will they sing to me?" Claire knew what Henry wanted.

She took the teddy bear from Henry and said, "How 'bout I sing to you now? Me and Baby."

Henry giggled. "Okay, will you sing the monkey song?"

Claire began the song, including all the hand motions and sound effects which caused Henry to yell, "Again!" when she neared the end.

The doorbell rang, sending Henry charging for the door. He got there before Claire had made it out of the bedroom.

Tossing the door open, Henry beamed at Kyle and Daisey. "Can we color dinosaurs again, Daisey?" Henry grabbed Daisey's hand and pulled her inside.

Kyle brought up the rear. "Looks like I'm going to have some tough competition tonight for Daisey's attention."

"Yes, he's been looking forward to this all day. According to him, Daisey loves coloring and dinosaurs and fire. I'm not sure if I should be worried about the last one."

Henry took Daisey and Kyle to his room to retrieve the Crayons and his assortment of coloring books while Claire went to her room to get her purse and the shawl and the list.

As she passed the mirror, she took one last look, pressing down a stray curl. When was the last time she had dressed for an occasion?

Pensacola.

There she sat in one of the nicest restaurants in town across from a brown-haired man with a strong chin and dancing blue eyes. It was the night she told Ryan she was expecting. He had been so excited. His face radiated with joy as he reached out to take her hand.

Once the baby was born, his excitement faded a little with each passing month. By the time Henry was one, they knew something wasn't right. At two, his diagnosis had been confirmed, and Ryan, well, he became absent, disappearing altogether like smoke on a cold day. He blew away.

Tonight's date was her first since her divorce over a year ago.

Claire sat on the edge of the bed. Panic seized her.

Her breathing came in small gasps. She pushed herself up and began to pace.

She shook her arms and rolled her shoulders, hoping to send the anxiety out of her body.

"What am I doing? I can't go out with Haden tonight. I'm supposed to be looking out for Henry's best interest. We're just going to get hurt." She explained to the woman in the mirror. "I've lost my mind."

"I know what'll happen. We're going to go out. He's going to kiss me again. My brain is going to be mush. I mean mush. He'll tell his mom it was all a lie, and I'm history. He'll fire me faster than a Texas twister. Who wants a lie hanging around?"

The doorbell chimed.

Claire stopped, standing stone still, looking to the woman in the mirror for help.

She heard the murmur of voices. A minute later, Daisey knocked on the door. "Claire, Haden's here."

Claire didn't answer.

"Are you alright?"

"I'm fine." Another lie. "I'm looking for Baby. If Henry doesn't have him at bedtime, he'll be scared."

As she reached for the bear on the bed, Claire remembered what Haden had said, something about being scared? He didn't figure her for a scaredy-cat. His words rang in her ears. The teasing tone, the smug look, the challenge that rose in his eyes, right before he kissed her.

"What nerve?" She wasn't about to give him the satisfaction of being right.

With determination coursing through her five feet two, with heels, frame, she pointed her finger at the woman in the reflection. "I'm not scared of Haden Sawyer!"

Chapter Eighteen

The Business Man's Annual Charity Ball took place in the Ole Riley Mansion up on the hill overlooking Miller Creek. Every year the staff of the mansion decorated the house with twinkling lights, polished all the silver, and literally rolled out the red carpet. It was one of the year's biggest events.

As they neared the long drive, the mansion gleamed in the distance. The lights hanging on its eaves glowed against the purple night sky. The place looked magical.

A lot like Claire, thought Haden. He glanced over at her. Her brunette hair hung in soft curls framing her face. Her green eyes shimmered set against the sky- blue dress she wore. It took all his will power not to reach over and pull her to him.

The entry way ended in a circular drive, and Haden pulled the truck in behind the last vehicle. A valet appeared. Haden handed him the keys and went around the truck to open the door for Claire.

"Your chariot has arrived." Haden bowed. He gave Claire his hand to help her down to the running board.

He caught the aroma of Claire's perfume as he offered her his arm. She clung to it. "I'm not use to heels. I'm more comfortable in sneakers."

Her confession acted as a balm to Haden's mind. "I know. This monkey suit feels likes its strangling me." He pulled at his tie with his right hand.

Claire stopped and turned, looking him over from head to toe.

"You clean up good." Her smile crept into her eyes.

A woman in a long taffeta gown swished by knocking against his leg. "I guess we better go in before we get run over."

"Yeah," said Claire, "We'd hate to stop traffic."

Haden gave Claire a knowing look. "That would be terrible."

Claire's eyes twinkled in response. He'd give anything to keep that twinkle there.

Haden opened the front door of the mansion and followed Claire into the foyer which had marble floors and two spiral staircases made of maple that ran the length of each wall.

Haden had attended enough of these events over the years to know the layout of the mansion. The living room and what would've been a parlor was on the right and acted as a dance floor. The library to their left was now a bar. The tables for the dinner dotted the floor of the formal dining hall, which could fit the two hundred or so guests without any problem.

He watched with amusement as Claire took it all in.

"This place is a palace. Henry said I looked like a princess; now, I feel like one."

"I did promise you a ball," He helped Claire out of her shawl. "Did you want to keep this with you?"

"No, I'll be fine." She passed him her purse, then stopped. "Would you mind holding onto my phone. I don't seem to have any pockets in my princess dress."

"I'd be happy to." Haden held her purse while she fished out her phone. "All done?"

"Yeah." Claire gave him the phone for safe keeping.

Haden handed the shawl and purse to the lady behind the counter at the coat closet. Turning, he walked back towards Claire tucking the claims ticket and Claire's phone in his inside jacket pocket.

Haden caught Claire's hand and intertwined their fingers. He liked having her close. He led her into the dance floor area where the musicians hustled to get set up. Everyone was milling around, chatting, waiting to be seated for dinner.

"Would you like something to drink?" He asked above the noise.

"That sounds great," Claire looked around the room. "I thought Adele and Jed were going to be here, too."

"They should be." Haden looked over the heads of those in the crowd and spotted Jed with his date Emma, the owner of the local bakery. "I see Jed and Emma, but I don't see Aunt Adele."

"It's alright. I'll find my way around. Why don't you go get those drinks?"

"Punch or something else."

"I better stick with punch. No sloshed princesses."

Haden winked and headed over to the library where the bar was located. The servers flung ice cubes into cups as quick as they could. Not worrying about spills, the liquor and the soda flowed.

Haden held up two fingers and indicated the punch. He handed the server a couple of dollars for his trouble.

When he turned around holding the two drinks, he found Sarah standing directly behind him. Haden didn't like the way she was looking at him. "Haden, you're looking yummy tonight." She grabbed his tie and pulled him out of the line.

Now, standing closer to her, he could smell her breath. “I see you’ve had a drink or two. Maybe, we should find your date.”

“I don’t want to find my date. I want to talk to you.” Sarah yanked on his tie.

“Okay, what do you want to talk about?” He shifted his weight while holding a drink in each hand and bending at the hips.

“I want to know why you let everybody think I was the one to call off the wedding. That wasn’t very nice of you.” She tsk-ed, wagging her finger in his general direction.

Haden tensed. “Well, I guess when you left, I thought it was easier. It’s what everyone assumed, so, I let them.”

“I want to be angry with you, but you’re such a cutie pie, I can’t be. I’ve missed you.” Her words slurred together as she leaned against him.

“I think we need to have this conversation some other time when you’re more yourself.” Haden tried to stand straight but couldn’t.

“I’m myself. Are you yourself? You look like yourself.” To Haden’s surprise, Sarah nuzzled up to him, pulled him closer by his tie and began to nibble his jawline. Haden balanced the cups, keeping the pink liquid from spilling all over her white gown, while trying to back away.

“Excuse me,” came a low rumbling voice. “I believe you have my date cornered.”

Haden struggled to turn his head, but Sarah tightened her grip on his tie. “There’s been a misunderstanding. I could use some help here,” Haden pleaded.

The other man walked around Haden to where he could see him.

He looked familiar, but Haden couldn't remember his name. "I think she's had a little too much to drink."

The other man gave Haden a sour look. "You think?"

With resignation, he pulled Sarah's hands from Haden's tie. Haden kept repeating, "Sorry."

"Come on Sarah, honey. We can be seated now." The man glared at Haden as he led her away.

Haden watched as Sarah left the room from one set of doors. When he turned, he found Claire standing in the doorway of the other set. Her arms crossed, looking like she might pop. Her lips clinched together tight.

Haden zig-zagged his way across the room. "Hi, one punch as ordered."

Claire glared at him from under her long lashes as she took the drink. Her green eyes bright with fire. "What did Sarah want?"

"Just to talk"

"Umm. It looked like a lot more than talking from where I stood." Claire sipped the punch.

"Well, it wasn't. She had a question, and I told her I thought we should talk about it some other time."

"Will that discussion also include her nibbling your chin?"

Haden froze, trying to figure out what to say and not wanting to dig a deeper hole when it hit him. "You're jealous."

"No…I'm not jealous. I have standards. I expect when a man takes me out he spends his time with me not his ex."

Haden leaned close to her ear, careful to keep his voice low. "Will you nibble my chin if I spend my time with you?"

Claire reddened. "Let's go find our seats."

∞

Claire leaned her chin in her hand as she listened to Adele. "You see the skinny guy with the jet-black hair? He's Calvin, and he has the best egg laying chickens this side of Tupelo. So, when I found out Tina made omelets, I knew it was a match made in heaven."

"Sounds more like it was made at Tyson Farms to me." Frank nudged Adele with his elbow.

Claire smothered a giggle. She loved Adele and didn't want to offend her. However, she considered Adele's love advice a little iffy at best.

Because of it, she had to sit through a meal with a man she knew was interested in someone else. Talk about a match made in heaven, Sarah was an architect, and he owned a construction company. Eggs and Omelets.

Yeah, she and Haden had kissed. So, what? And yes, it caused seizures of molten lava to move through her veins. But what was that really? Hormones.

He did look handsome in his navy-blue suit, though.

Claire let her gaze wander across the table to where he sat. She watched as he reached for his coffee, pulling his coat taunt over his broad shoulders. When he leaned back laughing at Frank's joke, her eyes caught his, and instead of turning away, she lingered in the chocolate depths of them, wading into their warmth. They looked sweeter than the dessert sitting in front of her.

He stood and came to her as if he had sensed her thoughts. Leaning close, he whispered, "Do you want to dance?"

His breath across her ear sent tingles down her arms. If she turned her head, she could brush his lips with hers. What would he think if she did?

"Yes," she answered.

He took her hand, leading her to the dance floor. The live band played an assortment of forties and fifties melodies, everything from swing to sock hop.

Couples moved in time with the beats. Jed and his date glided past them as they found a spot on the dance floor.

Haden drew her into his arms; she placed her hand on his shoulder, keeping a respectable distance between them.

Claire relaxed once they had made a few turns around the floor. "You're a good dancer."

"Surprised?"

"A little. I didn't figure it was a necessary skill for a construction worker."

"It is if your last name is Sawyer. Mom made us all take ballroom dancing when we were kids. Ever the romantic. She thought it might come in handy." Heat entered Haden's eyes. "She was right."

Claire ignored the desire she heard thick in his voice. She didn't want to melt into his warm touch or give in to the feel of his strong arms around her. She was afraid. He had been right.

Then, they played Misty.

As the music floated over the room, she fell into a magical spell. The distance between them shortened until her head was on his shoulder. Her eyes drifted close as they swayed together. She could hear him humming along with the song.

"Claire?"

"Umm," she answered without opening her eyes.

"I want to kiss you, again. But I don't want to confuse you."

"Umm, how thoughtful." she murmured.

Before she could say anything else, Haden's lips brushed hers. Without thinking, she caught his lower lip, urging him to deepen the kiss, and there in front of every Tom, Dick, and Adele, Claire welcomed Haden into her heart.

With his hand in the small of her back, Haden pressed her closer to him. She moved her hand to the back of his neck, catching a soft brown curl in her finger tips.

The music changed; the spell burst.

Claire pulled back first. Questions swirled in her head.

She couldn't read Haden's face, but his hands held her waist. Before she could say anything, she heard her name being called.

Haden dropped his hands as she turned towards the voice. "Claire, Claire…" She spotted Kyle as he weaved his way through the crowd to reach them. "You've got to come home. Somethings wrong with Henry."

Chapter Nineteen

Haden threw the truck into park. Before he could get around to help Claire out, she bolted, leaving the door hanging open.

Daisey stepped aside and swung the screen door wide, allowing Claire to zip past into the house. Haden shut the truck door and jogged to the porch, letting the screen door banged shut.

"What happened? Where is he? Did he get sick to his stomach?"

"He's okay. He did get sick to his stomach, but we got him cleaned up. He's settled on the couch with a cold, wet rag watching a movie."

"Oh, thank goodness."

Haden stepped behind her. "I'll take your things."

Claire pulled the wrap from around her and dropped it into his arms. The purse she flung on top of the wrap.

As Haden laid the mound on the table in the entrance, Claire moved towards Henry.

"He's running a bit of a fever, though, so we decided to come get you," said Daisey, following her.

"Why didn't you call? We would've come right home. When Kyle showed up in person, I assumed the worst."

"We did, but nobody answered. After the third try, we decided Kyle should go get you. I mean we did say we'd contact you if there was a problem."

Claire reached out and put her hand on the younger woman's

shoulder. "You guys did great."

Claire sat beside Henry, who was lost in the movie and eased her hand into his as the ogre on the screen burst out into song.

"Kyle was so worried we'd broken Henry." Daisey said to Haden. "You should've seen him when Henry got sick in the kitchen. He almost lost it. He freaked when we couldn't get a hold of Claire."

"It's my fault," said Haden. "I put both phones in my coat pocket on vibrate. I guess they were buried too deep."

Claire raised her hand to Henry's forehead. She looked towards Haden and Daisey and nodded. She pulled Henry towards her and let him rest his head on her lap, laying the cool rag across his brow. The bathroom trash can sat at his feet.

Kyle bustled in, closing the front door behind him. "Wow, you made great time. I didn't know that ole pick-up could fly."

"It's amazing what you can do when you have a worried Mama in the vehicle." Haden chuckled. "I think you scared the day lights out of her when you showed up."

"Yeah, sorry about that. How is he?" Kyle directed his question to Daisey. She came to him.

"He's settled in for now, but we were right; he does have a fever." Daisey wrapped her arms around Kyle as he slipped his right arm around her shoulders.

"Look, how about I pay for a trip to Burger Express for the two of you. You can stop on the way home. There's no sense in you guys hanging around here."

"Maybe, I wanted to see if the ogre gets the girl."

Daisey elbowed Kyle in the ribs. "You know he does. Take the money for the food."

"I've got money," said Kyle into her hair as he planted a kiss among her blonde curls.

Haden rolled his eyes. "Think of it as a reward for a job well done." Haden got his wallet out and pulled two tens from the sleeve.

Daisey snatched them from his hand. "Kyle might be shy about taking the money, but I'm a poor college student with a minimum wage part-time job, who could use a big fat juicy burger."

"And fries," added Kyle.

After they left, Haden closed and locked the front door. After seeing Claire panic the way she had, Haden planned to stay with her. No way, was he letting her go through tonight alone.

He joined Claire and Henry in the living room to see if he could help.

"Can I get you anything, sport?" The boy turned his head in Haden's direction and shook it. "How about you? Want anything from the kitchen?"

"Would you mind bringing me the notebook on the kitchen table? It's blue with colorful bubbles on the cover. And a pen."

"Sure, no problem."

Haden figured the notebook would be a no brainer to find. However, the kitchen table doubled as a desk with stacks and piles and mounds. "This looks like the trailer."

"What?" called Claire from the living room.

"Nothing, talking to myself."

He rummaged around, hoping the notebook would jump out at him.

As he dug, he started counting the menagerie of medical bills. His heart ached. Claire had so much on her. If he could get hold of her ex right now, he'd throttle him, within an inch of his life, twice. How could a man leave his wife, the mother of his child, to deal with this?

He stood in the kitchen long enough to get a handle on his frustration.

When Haden entered the living room, he held the notebook, pen, and a cup of water for Henry.

"I know if you get sick to your stomach, you should hydrate. So, I brought Henry some water." Haden handed the notebook and pen to Claire. Sitting on the other side of Henry, he lifted him onto his lap. Henry didn't even flinch. Haden handed him the small plastic cup, and Henry drank a few sips.

Claire sat dumb struck. "I can't believe you got him to cooperate."

"What do ya mean? Henry and I are buds. We both like trucks. Right man?"

"Yeah," answered Henry. "Mom said one day I could come see your trucks."

"I think we can make it happen. How about when you get to feeling better next week I'll take you and your mom to one of the sites and you can see them in action. Would you like that?"

"Yep. Can I bring Baby?" Haden looked to Claire for an explanation. She mouthed the words teddy bear.

"Sure, Baby needs to be there." Henry snuggled into Haden's

shoulder. "You got a blanket?" He asked Claire.

"Sure," She sprang from her seat to pull the throw from the back of the chair which sat cattycornered to the couch.

After tossing the blanket over the two of them, Claire excused herself to go to change and get the thermometer.

Haden and Henry watched the ogre defeat the short man winning the maidens heart. If only it were that simple.

He looked down to find Henry asleep. The sound of his soft breath made Haden relax; before he knew it, his head bobbed forward, causing him to jerk awake.

Claire giggled. "Don't break your neck."

Haden turned to find Claire snuggled up under the blanket with them. She had changed and now wore an old red tee-shirt and sweat pants in place of the sparkling blue dress. Her eyes shined like emeralds.

"I must've drifted off. Did you get everything into the notebook?"

"As much as I could. Henry's been having some stomach issues the last few weeks. I've been trying to keep a food diary. The doctors think it might be allergies, but…" Claire's face tightened; her jaw tensed.

"But what?"

"Let's not talk about it now."

"Why not? I'm interested." Haden looked down at Henry. The feel of the little boy in his arms stirred the need to protect him. "What else could it be?"

"They're not sure, but they want to do some more tests." Claire looked at her hands in her lap.

Haden saw the fear on her face; he watched as the tears began to form. "He's been through so much already." She reached out and took Henry's small hand in hers. "I'm not sure I can go through much more, watching him in pain, bracing myself every time we go to the doctors, waiting for them to pronounce the next hurtle." Claire stammered as the tears began to roll down her cheeks. She swiped them away with her free hand.

Haden's heart wrenched. He wrapped his free arm around her, drawing her to him. She nuzzled her head into his shoulder, fighting the tears and losing.

∞

The volume of the car salesman promising 'the best prices of the season' on the TV jarred Claire awake.

She rolled from her side onto her back and flung her arm over her eyes, trying to get comfortable. When the cushion under her head moved, she lowered her arm and looked straight up into Haden Sawyer's nostrils.

She froze. Not sure she was seeing right, she blinked. Nope, it was nose hairs, and along a very masculine jawline, stubble.

With the stealth of a cat in a china shop, Claire eased her head from Haden's lap but couldn't dislodge herself from his arm. The last thing she remembered, she was sobbing into his shirt.

Haden had wrapped her in one arm while he held a sleeping Henry in the other and let her cry. Afterwards, she rested her head on his chest and the rhythmic beating of his heart along with the warmth of his body had calmed her. Maybe, a little too much.

As she lifted his hand from her shoulder, she attempted to stand. Haden mumbled something and drew her back to his body. She tried to fight it but couldn't keep her balance. She wound up plopping back onto the couch, sure she had awakened both Haden and Henry.

Claire assessed her situation and decided to use Haden as a brace. She would place her hand on Haden's thigh in order to push herself up and out of his hold, hoping as she slipped out of his arm it would drop to his side.

Instead of planting her right hand in the needed spot, she wound up sliding it into place. She turned her body, putting her at an odd angle and causing Haden to roll to his left and reach across her with his right arm, trapping her. His head rested on her shoulder where he nuzzled into her hair.

Now what was she supposed to do?

"You smell like lavender."

Claire jumped clean off the couch, stumbling over the discarded blanket and landing on her rear in the middle of the living room floor.

"You dirty rat. You were awake the whole time."

"Not the whole time, but when you started running your hand over my thigh…Well, that woke me up." Claire saw the heat in his eyes and knew she'd better change the subject.

"Henry's out cold. I better put him to bed."

"Point the way, and I'll carry him for you."

"No, it's okay. I can manage."

"I know you can manage, but you don't have to. Let me carry the little man."

"Okay but watch his head as you go down the hall." Claire pushed herself up from the floor to lead the way.

Haden stood and gathered Henry into his arms. "He still feels warm."

It amazed Claire how easy Haden could lift and carry Henry. She struggled with him even though he was small for his age. Henry looked right at home in Haden's arms, the same way she had felt when he held her.

How could any woman in their right mind leave a man like Haden standing at the altar?

"I'll be sure to keep an eye on his temperature through the night."

"So, do you often whack Henry's head as you carry him down the hall?"

Claire turned, stopping in front of Henry's bedroom door. "I can't believe you asked that. Are you calling my parenting abilities into question?"

A smile appeared on Haden's face letting his dimples loose and crinkling the corners of his eyes. "Hold up, Mama bear. I'm asking because of your remark about watching his head."

Claire shrugged, "I might be speaking from experience, but I'm a quick learner. The hallways were wider in our home back in Florida." Claire leaned her body against the door jamb.

"Is that where you lived before moving to the Great State of Alabama?"

"Yeah, I loved the beach and the people, but once the divorce went through, there were too many memories for me. So, we packed up and came to the country."

"Why here? Family?"

"No, more like a specialist for Henry and a job for me." Claire shrugged. "But once I started the job, they realized the amount of time I needed to take off for Henry. They let me go."

"Well, I'm glad they did, or I wouldn't have met you." A look swept across his face, and he moved closer to her.

Henry shifted in Haden's arms.

"He must be getting heavy." Claire moved into the bedroom, slipped past Haden and turned on the lamp that sat on the bedside table. To put distance between them, she moved around the twin bed, pulling down the comforter and sheet.

Haden followed her into the room. With great care, he placed Henry's head on the pillow and pulled up the covers. Seeing Baby propped by the headboard, he tucked the toy under the covers right beside Henry.

Haden stood back, gazing down at the sleeping child. Claire couldn't help herself. The care that crept into Haden's eyes as he looked at her son made her want to throw her arms around him and never let go.

This sudden thought scared her. She didn't know him. All the jumbled feelings from earlier raced back into her mind. Her gaze met his, and the fears faded.

He leaned over and turned out the lamp, leaving them standing in the dark.

Haden took her hand, moving it to his lips. The warmth as he kissed the back of her hand sent sweet tingles all over her. He tugged her to him and placed his left hand on the base of her back. His breath on her cheek invited her to wrap her arms around his neck as he touched his lips to hers.

"You need to stop doing this"

“Doing what?”

“Kissing me, confusing me. I don’t have room for you.” Haden listened while nibbling her ear. She let out a sigh in spite of her protest.

“This house has plenty of room and so does mine.” Claire pushed away from him.

“You know that’s not what I mean.”

Henry rustled beneath his covers. Haden took Claire’s hand and led her out into the hall, closing the door behind her. The hall light glowed a quiet yellow.

“No need to wake him,” Haden’s whisper sounded husky and raw as he drew Claire closer.

In the light, she saw things clearer. She pulled away but kept a hold of his hand. “Here let me walk you out.” She moved him into the living room. She hoped this would have a cold-water effect on him. She needed to slow things down. Her heart wanted all Haden was offering, but her head shouted ‘No’. Loud and Clear.

Haden stopped dead in the middle of the living room. “I’m not going anywhere until we get this settled. I know you’re drawn to me, and I’ve made it clear how I feel about you. So, what’s got you so confused?”

“Other than this is all a lie?” Claire dropped his hand and crossed her arms.

“That’s not what it is now. Does it matter how it started?”

“Yes, it matters to me. You can’t build a life on a lie. I’ve already tried; it doesn’t work.”

Chapter Twenty

Haden rolled down the windows and cranked up the music on his drive to church Sunday. Claire's words from the other night played in his mind. It was true. Their relationship had been a mere fabrication for his mother's sake, but couldn't she see things had changed.

His feelings were real, so real they surprised him. He slammed the palm of his hand against the steering wheel.

He stabbed at the CD button on the dash. He needed quiet. As he settled back into his seat, smelling the scent of spring wildflowers, the image of Claire in her red tee-shirt and ratty sweat pants popped into his mind. She had made her position crystal clear Friday night. She wanted everything out in the open. No more lies.

Haden cringed.

He knew coming clean about their relationship wasn't the only thing he needed to set straight with his family. Sarah had called him on the wedding mess at the Businessman's Charity Ball.

A knot began to form in the pit of his stomach.

Haden pulled his truck into a spot outside of the First Community Church. He took a moment to roll up the windows before cutting the engine.

Pulling down the visor, he checked his hair in the mirror. He ran his fingers through it trying to subdue the tangled mass. Studying his face, he asked, "When did you become such a liar?" He pushed the visor out of his way, disappointed with himself.

The question dug around in his brain as his eyes alit on the Bible sitting next to him on the seat; the Bible his father had given him. Touching the soft leather, he recalled the time when he was twelve and his dad caught him lying to his mom about a broken picture frame. The frame held an old black and white of his grandmother that hung on the wall in the hall. He and Kyle had been throwing the basketball in the house, which they knew was against the rules.

The instant the picture hit the floor Kyle took off for home, leaving Haden to face the blame alone.

When his mom asked him about it, he denied it was him; lied.

By the time his dad got home, he'd dug himself in pretty deep.

"Son," his father had said, "Let me tell you something about being a man. It's not what you look like on the outside or what you own that makes you one; it's who you are on the inside. And lying, that's not the way."

Haden sunk deep into his seat and folded his hands over his middle, letting those words settle into his heart. A few minutes later, Haden spotted Jed jogging towards him across the parking lot.

"You coming in or are you going to listen to the sermon on the radio?" Jed opened the door of the truck for him. Haden reached over and grabbed his Bible and his keys.

"I'm coming."

"You look about as miserable as a kid with no cake at a birthday party. What's eating you?" Jed closed the door as he and Haden fell into step.

"Claire." Haden knew the moment her name left his lips he shouldn't have brought it up with Jed.

Jed stopped. "What've you done now?" His jaw tightened as he glared at Haden.

"I didn't do anything. It's more what I haven't done." Haden started walking towards the church. He waved to Charlie Lee, the president of the Businessman's League, and his wife as they herded their kids towards the building.

Jed grabbed his arm, stepping in front of him. "Hold up. Don't talk in circles. What's going on with you and Claire?"

"I don't want to talk about it, all right. Besides, it's none of your business anyway." Haden tried to move past him, but Jed blocked the sidewalk. Jed might be taller by an inch or two and broader across the shoulders, but Haden had no doubts he could take him.

"You got that dead wrong, brother." Jed poked him in the chest. "Claire works for us, and if you run her off, we all suffer, and to be clear, last time I looked Betty Sawyer was my mom too. Our mom who you lied to. So, don't give me any of that bull about it not being my business. When all this blows-up in your face, it'll be me helping you clean it up." Jed stood straight with his arms crossed.

So much for the balm of family solace. "You're right. You've been there for me."

"You know it. Who had your back after Sarah left you?"

Haden's heart sank. "You." There was no escaping the lies.

"Now, what's going on between you and Claire?"

"Things got revved up after Kyle and Daisey left Friday night."

Haden thumped his Bible against his hip.

Jed's brow creased. "How revved up?"

"Nothing like that. Geez. Give me some credit." Haden pushed past Jed and marched to the glass doors. He opened them and entered, with Jed close on his heels.

Jed grabbed Haden by the arm again.

"If you don't stop, I'm gonna level you right here," said Haden.

But Jed didn't let go.

"Look," said Jed in a low tone. "Revved up, not revved up, I don't care. But Claire's been through enough with her ex-husband leaving her and with Henry's condition. You better be sure, rock solid sure, before you go any further."

Adele poked her head out the door of the worship auditorium. "Come on you two quit clowning around. We've got seats up front."

Jed released Haden's arm and followed Adele into the worship center without glancing back.

Haden, clutching his Bible, stood contemplating whether to go in or make a run for it.

"Haden, Haden," he heard a voice calling. He turned around and saw Henry bounding for him full speed.

He squatted, and the boy stopped himself by falling into his arms. "Hey, sport. You're feeling better."

"Yes, and you know what that means, right?"

Haden wracked his brain. "No, what does it mean?" Claire appeared hauling a backpack, her Bible and notebook, a purse, and a foam cup of coffee.

"The trucks, the trucks," Henry began to chant.

"I'm sorry. I tried to catch him, but when he saw you, he took off."

Haden looked up at Claire. She wore a hot pink dress that gave her complexion a warm glow. Her brunette hair laid soft around her shoulders.

"It's alright." He turned his attention back to the child in his arms. "So, you're feeling better."

"Yes sir, I'm normal." Henry stood tall with his chest out.

"That's better than I can say," chuckled Haden. "When should we go see the trucks?"

"Mom? Today?"

"Oh, I don't know, but not today. We don't want to take up Haden's day off." Claire shifted from one foot to the other. Haden enjoyed seeing her squirm. "Maybe I should check our calendar…to make sure we don't have any doctor appointments or something."

Claire looked at him with pleading eyes. He didn't want to give her any help; he wanted to spend time with her and Henry, but he owed her. "How about this? We give your mom time to look at her calendar, and instead, you two plan on going with me to the little league baseball game Friday night. We can cheer for Kyle's team, the Yellow Hammers."

"Isn't that a bird?" asked Claire.

Haden stood. "It's the state bird, but Kyle thought the hammer part was a good fit with the construction company thing." He gave her a lop-sided grin.

Claire smiled, and it spread all the way to her eyes. "He does have a point."

The usher came through the wooden doors that led into the

worship center, and they could hear the congregation singing, "Jesus paid it all, all to Him I owe…"

"We'd better go in," said Claire as she adjusted her load.

"Come on Haden." Henry grasped Haden's hand and pulled him to the doors. Claire followed behind.

"Here, let's help your mom." Haden released Henry and took the notebook. He passed it to Henry who hugged it to his chest. Then he took her Bible and added it to his before grabbing the coffee cup. Holding everything in one hand, he opened the door to the auditorium allowing Claire to enter first.

There they stood, the three of them, together. Haden heard Jed's words. "You better be rock solid sure."

Haden took Henry's hand and lead the boy to the front where his own mother and aunt were sitting. Claire slipped into the pew behind them, followed by Henry and Haden. Jed turned and shot Haden a frosty look.

Once the preacher started his message, Haden leaned over Henry and whispered into Claire's ear. "You never did answer. Will you go with me to the game Friday night?"

"Why? It's not real. I can't keep pretending, not even for your mom." Claire leaned back in her seat and folded her hands in her lap.

Haden scooted closer, causing Henry to lean against his chest. "It's a real date. I'm asking you out on a real date."

Claire studied his face. Now, he knew why organisms under a microscope squirmed. "Will you?" He asked a second time his tone taking on an edge.

"A real date."

Haden clenched his jaw tight. "Please."

"A real date."

"Yes," his voice rose. "Why is that so hard to believe?"

Claire touched his leg, her eyes wide. Haden looked around and found his mother looking back at him. She put her finger to her lips, shushing him and rolled her eyes. A small wave of shuffling washed through the pews around him.

He moved Henry into his lap and placed his arm across the back of the pew behind Claire. "Let's start again." He whispered in her ear. "Let's go on a real date and start again."

"What about the lie?"

"As soon as the surgery is over, I'll tell her."

Claire cut her eyes in his direction. "Don't you mean we?"

"No, I'll talk to her. It's my mess; I'll clean it up. Will you give this a chance?"

Haden's heart thrummed in his chest.

"I'll think about it. The date. I'll think about the date."

Before service dismissed, the preacher lead everyone in a special prayer for his mother, asking for safety during Tuesday's surgery and a full recovery.

Haden sat recounting his morning as several of the more mature ladies gathered around Betty, making plans to bring meals. As he thought about it, he couldn't ever remember church being this hard or this thrilling.

∞

Claire paced around the small trailer. She had left instructions with Haden, Jed, and Kyle to call the minute Betty was out of surgery. She figured if she told all three of them it tripled her chances of actually hearing something.

The surgery was scheduled for eight, but Claire, a pro at dealing with the medical community, knew all too well that time meant nothing. Between Betty's surgery and the call that she had received from Henry's doctor, her mind was full.

Haden sent a text around nine thirty that they had taken Betty back to the operating room. Now, her watch read eleven. She picked up her phone to check; nothing. She made sure the volume was on high.

In order to distract herself, she filed.

The alphabet should have been easy enough but thoughts of Haden wove themselves into her work. A is for avoiding him on purpose Saturday after the events of Friday night. B is for brown chocolate eyes. C is for crying in his arms. It's hard to be snarky with someone who let you cry all over their shirt, twice.

She took in a deep breath, remembering the smell of his cologne, another C word. How his shoulders broad, that would be under B as well, and strong – S- had carried Henry to bed. The darkness and the kisses. K might be her favorite letter of all.

She fanned herself with one of the files before stuffing it in and slamming the drawer shut. This wasn't helping.

The urge to go to Adele's café and talk things over with her about 'the real date' was strong, but she knew Adele was at the hospital. Family first. She liked that about the Sawyers.

A real date. No lie to keep up. They'd be going because they wanted to be with each other, not to keep up appearances. The fact that Henry was part of the date made her heart long for Haden more.

Haden didn't mind having Henry around; in fact, she knew he loved it. His patience and gentleness with her son won him some big brownie points in her mom book. That was the thing, his care for Henry was genuine. It was his feelings for her she doubted.

She sat down with a thud unable to take in the idea.

"It's not about Henry," she said out loud. "It's about me."

Her cell phone rang.

"Hey, Mom's out." The joy in Haden's voice raced across the line. "The doctors think they got it all, and the reconstruction went fine." He paused. "They'll do blood work to see where her cancer markers fall. But they're confident after chemo she'll be cancer free."

"Oh, Haden, that's marvelous. I wish I could be there when she wakes up, but someone has to hold down the fort."

"Yeah, I wish you could be here, too." Claire heard the need for her in his voice. It unnerved her.

"Oh, before I forget. I wanted to let you know Sarah stopped by yesterday and today, looking for you. I meant to tell you yesterday, but we never crossed paths."

"No, I needed to be outside yesterday; if I had stayed in the office, I would've been worse than a caged animal," said Haden.

"I thought about leaving a sticky note on your computer screen, but I know how much you love that."

Claire relished the fact they had their own private jokes.

Haden chuckled. "You got that right. Did Sarah say what she wanted?" Claire thought she caught a hint of worry in his words.

"Not really. I assumed she wanted an update on your mom. I told her what I could."

"Great, thanks. Look, I know this isn't the best time, but..."

"Why is it people say that, and yet, they still continue on with what they were going to say?" Claire hoped to steer the conversation a different direction. "like I know you just broke your arm, but can I ask you to rake the yard. I mean if you already know it's a bad time or the wrong time why ask?"

"Claire, I'm gonna ask." Haden's tone went flat.

Rats. "No, I haven't decided about the ball game Friday night. Henry's been having some stomach trouble, as you know, and the doctors have decided to do some tests."

"What kind of tests?"

"Blood work and an Upper and Lower G.I. scope. They want to rule out some possibilities."

"Do you know what they're looking for?" asked Haden.

"Again, like you said this probably isn't the best time." Claire doodled on the sticky pad in front of her while she talked. "I don't want to ruin your good news."

"Tell me."

"I'd rather not." Claire looked down and saw the rows of hearts. She dropped the pen.

"Look, you know I'm not going to let this go, so make this easy on both of us and tell me."

"They think it might be Crohn's disease. It's something that can happen to kids with Juvenile Dermatomyositis. So, they keep an eye out for it. They want to do the tests next Wednesday." Claire couldn't keep the pain from rippling into her voice.

"I'll get Kyle to cover the office, so we can both be there. I know this is a setback. Are you going to be okay?"

"Again, something people say when they already know the answer." Claire bit her lip. She didn't mean to be so snarky. Her heart sat shattered at her feet along with her hopes for Henry's remission. "I'm sorry. I'm just so tired of the hurdles. We make it over one, and then another one pops up. It's like I'm on a roller coaster ride with my hands in the air, screaming, but the loop never ends."

Chapter Twenty-one

Haden pushed the disconnect button, wanting to be in two places at once.

He needed to stay until his mother got settled into a room, but his heart longed to comfort Claire.

He paced, willing the time to pass. The others sat in the waiting room to his left entertaining themselves.

Why had he asked such a stupid question? Of course, she wasn't okay. She fought to be okay every day, for Henry. She bore the burden of a child with a life-threatening disease, and she did it alone.

Now, he got what Jed had been saying.

Claire wasn't a woman you could try on and see if she fit. You couldn't wear her when you needed a plus one at some fancy event like a good suit. No, she needed someone who was all in for the long haul, not simply for her but for Henry.

She needed a rock-solid surety that when she turned around, he'd be there.

The nurse came from behind two large doors that parted automatically for her. Haden spotted her from down the hall and hurried over to her. "Mr. Sawyer, your mother is awake now and is being moved to a room."

"Oh, that's great." Relief flooded through him.

"She'll be on the fourth floor in room 407. If you'll give us a few minutes to get her settled, you should be able to see her."

"How long do you think it will take?"

The nurse looked at her watch. "Oh, give us about ten minutes." Turning, she disappeared once more behind the two automated doors. Haden pulled out his phone to note the time.

He joined the rest of his family in the waiting room. Aunt Adele had taken charge of his mother's possessions. Two plastic bags containing clothes, shoes, and the latest mystery by Anne Donna sat in one of the cloth seats. At Adele's feet sat two large purses, one black with fraying straps and one coral with gold rings adorning the front pocket.

When Haden entered, everyone looked up. "The nurse said Mom's awake."

A ripple of relief ran through the small room as everyone started putting their books and phones away. Adele clapped her hands. "Yes, praise the Lord." She stood to heft the two purses into a chair of their own.

"They asked if we could give them about ten minutes, so they could get her settled in the room before we all go up."

"What's her room number?" Jed asked.

"407"

"407," repeated Adele.

Jed stretched. "I'm going to get a soda from the machine. Anyone want anything?"

"I'll walk with you," said Frank.

Adele had insisted on closing the café. "Family's family," she had said, and it had made perfect sense. It's what Lars and Otis would've done.

"I'll head on up with these bags and Mom's purse." Haden offered.

For a moment, he thought his aunt was going to protest, but he saw her eyeing the purses that sat in front of her. "That's a good idea. I'll call Kyle and let him know his Aunt Betty's out of recovery and what her room number is." Haden hated that Kyle needed to work. The Thomas project had fallen weeks behind, so Kyle had volunteered to oversee the site while he and Jed were at the hospital.

He walked over and lifted the corral purse. His arm gave way under its weight. He hoisted the purse onto his shoulder with a bounce and wrapped his arms around the two, full plastic bags. "I'll see you up there."

Haden held tight to the bags as he walked to the elevator.

An older gentleman pressed the elevator buttons for him, and he squeezed in before the doors closed. Haden caught the man eyeing him. "My mom had surgery." He offered, "these are her things." The gentleman nodded and looked straight ahead.

Feeling uncomfortable toting the monster of a purse, he plastered a smile on his lips and forged on.

Once he found the room, he was kept at bay by the closed door.

After a minute or two, a blonde-haired nurse swung it open. "You may go in, now." She said as she walked past him.

His mother looked so small in the hospital bed. He didn't like how it swallowed her up. "Hey, sweetheart. Look, I made it." Her eyes shined even though her lids threatened to close.

"Yes, I see." He placed the contents of his arms on one end of the blue sofa that sat parallel to the bed.

Turning, he took her hand in his.

"Where is everyone?" She asked her voice croaky.

"Downstairs. They'll be up in a minute." Haden pulled out his phone to check the time.

"Do you have some where you need to be?" She clasped his hand tighter and closed her eyes.

He leaned in and gave her a kiss on her forehead without letting go of her hand. "No, I'm right where I'm needed most."

"Did Claire come?"

"No, she thought it would be best if she stayed at the office and ran interference. I called and let her know you were out of surgery, though."

Betty half opened her eyes. "That's good. She's such a dear."

Haden sneaked a peek at his phone's screen again.

His mother squeezed his hand. "What's going on. You've been distracted for days. What is it?"

"You mean besides my mom having surgery?" He tried to make light of the situation, but his mother frowned.

"Yes, besides that."

Haden sat on the side of the bed. His stomach churned. He knew this was his opportunity to come clean. It presented itself to him like an open door. All he had to do was walk through it. "There's something I've been needing to tell you, but I didn't want you to be disappointed."

Betty sighed. "Oh, I'd never be disappointed in you. You've done so much for me since your father's death. I know I can depend on you. You're my rock."

"I wouldn't be so sure." Haden looked down at his hand holding her smaller one. Before he lost his nerve, he said, "Mom, I lied to you."

"I know."

Haden cocked his head, thinking he had misheard her. "No, I don't think you understand. I lied about Claire and me dating. I mean, I didn't even know her a month ago. The first time I met her, she yelled at me for holding up traffic, and that was the day before I interviewed her for the job."

"I know."

Haden looked into his mom's eyes and saw love looking back at him. "Sweetie, a mother knows when her children are lying. It's like this sixth sense that God gives us, to help us out along the way. I knew when you introduced us, that she was no more your girlfriend than the man in the moon."

"So why did you let me go on with it?"

"Because I figured you had your reasons. I thought Sarah being back in town might be one. She was there that day." His mom shrugged. "Besides, your Aunt Adele's known Claire for about a year and has thought for some time you two would be good for one another."

Haden scowled. "You did this all in the name of matchmaking?"

"To be fair, you're the one who stuck his feet in the water. All I did was push." She smacked her lips together. "Could I have a sip of water? Talking has made me thirsty. My throat is so dry." She laid back in the bed and wiggled into a nook in the pillow.

Haden placed her hand on the bed and went to the night stand to get the small plastic jug filled with water.

"There's something else I need to tell you."

"Oh dear, what else?"

"Well, since you seem to be psychic, you may already know this too." He paused to pour the water into a foam cup and hunt for a straw. "Sarah isn't the one who called off our wedding. It was me."

His mother's head snapped towards him, nearly knocking out her oxygen tube. "You? But why?"

"We came to a place where we wanted different things." He poked the straw into the hole, making a funny noise.

"Like what, if I might ask? I liked Sarah. We had grown close. Why didn't you discuss this with me?"

Haden heard the hurt in her voice. "I knew you'd take it hard, so I let you think Sarah had dumped me. It was easier if everyone thought she had made the call."

"Well yeah!" With the strain on her voice, his mom began to cough. The pain played on her face. He gave her a sip of water to ease it. She took the cup from him and took a long drink through the straw. She smacked her lips again as she leaned back for a moment, scowling at him. "So, what were the differences?"

He stuck his hands in his pockets. "There were several, but the one I couldn't get past was that she didn't want to have children."

"You mean not right away or ever?"

"Ever or at least that's what she said then." He pulled his phone out of his pocket and looked at the time once more.

"Where do you need to be?" she asked as she handed him back the white foam cup.

"Claire got some bad news about Henry."

Betty's features softened at the mention of the child. "Henry's so adorable. I hate he's having to go through this."

"Yeah me too. That's why I need to go. Claire needs somebody to be there. She doesn't need to do it all alone. Not anymore."

Betty closed her eyes, smiling. "You care about her and Henry."

"Yes, I do. To be honest, I love her, but I'm pretty sure she doesn't feel the same. I mean after all, I dragged her into a lie. I can only imagine what she thinks of me. Besides, Jed has his eye on her, and she seems to care for him, too." Haden clenched his jaw.

Betty's eyes fluttered open. "I knew it. I knew you were falling for her. Every time you get around her, this silly in love grin appears. There's no hiding when you're in love. As for what she thinks about you, that's pretty clear as well."

"I don't know. She and Jed have a chemistry."

"Anybody home?" Jed entered the room followed by everyone else.

"Come on in." Betty shot Haden a warning look.

"What've you been up to Betty. I can recognize mischief on you when I see it." Adele looked at Haden, "Has she been trying to get up already? You didn't let her, did you?"

"No, ma'am. She's been as good as gold." Haden held his hands up in surrender.

"I better keep a close eye on you for the next few days. You've never been a good patient."

"Look, I've got to go," Haden said more for everyone else's sake than for Betty. He leaned over and planted another peck on her forehead. "I love you, Mom. Try to get some rest and no mischief."

"I will, dear. And don't worry. I understand." She patted his hand on the bed beside her. From the softness in her tone and the love in her eyes, he knew he was forgiven. Now, if he could get Claire to forgive him for the lie, he might get the chance to show her the truth of his love. Maybe there was a way.

∞

Haden crawled into the cab of his truck. He could see the sun low in the sky and knew it was after three. He so badly wanted to rush to Claire and comfort her and tell her he'd straightened everything out with his mom. But he had a plan, and he needed to get a few things first.

He inserted his key into the ignition, but before he cranked the engine, he spied his Bible laying on the floor. It had fallen open, and the thin pages were crumpled. Stretching over the console, he picked it up.

He flipped to the wrinkled pages and began pressing his hands across them to straighten them out. As he did, his eye landed on the heading Ten Commandments. He couldn't help but skim them. When his eyes reached the verse, "Do not steal. Do not deceive or cheat one another," his palms began to sweat. A gnawing feeling began to grow in the pit of his stomach. He laid the Bible aside and wiped his hands on his jeans.

"I know I've lied, but deceive?" He asked the roof of his truck. But the impulse wouldn't leave. The gnawing grew, and an image of Sarah popped into his mind. Yes, deceived. Haden groaned.

He glanced at the Bible then closed his eyes.

For the first time in a long time, Haden Sawyer prayed. It came out simple and to the point. *"Lord, help me. I need to straighten out this mess with everyone. I love Claire and Henry. Please forgive me. I know I don't deserve it, but I guess that's why I need it."*

Forty-five minutes later, He was on his way to Claire's house. The ice cream sat next to him on the seat of his truck. The clock on the dash read four. He had called the office, but no one answered. He figured Claire had gone home early after all the emotional tension of the day.

His mom was right about his feelings for her. They worked to keep him hopeful, but he knew that the situation was going to require more than an apology. She needed proof. Thanks to that no-account ex-husband, leaving.

The thought of Henry sleeping in his arms filled his mind. The sweet gentle snores. The boys frame small and light. Picking him up had been like picking up cotton balls.

How could any man in his right mind…?

Haden pulled into Claire's driveway. He could only imagine what she thought of him. Asking her to help him fool his own mother. Now, he'd have to win the trust of a woman who had every reason to doubt him.

He rang the bell and waited. The bag he held contained ice cream which was beginning to soften. He heard movement behind the door and assumed she was looking out the peephole.

"What are you doing here?" She called through the door.

"I came over to see how you and Henry are doing. I thought you could use some cheering up. So, I brought ice cream." Haden spied Claire's neighbor, Mrs. Clark watering her plants. He waved. She nodded.

"Why aren't you with your mother? She needs you right now." Her voice sounded further away. He cocked his head to listen.

"She has a band of nurses and family to take care of her." Haden frowned at the door. "Are you going to let me in or are we going to let the neighbors be part of this conversation?" He glanced in Mrs. Clark's direction, who turned her back to him.

"Besides the ice cream is melting."

There was no answer. Before he could say anything else, he heard a scraping noise, followed by Claire letting out a howl of pain.

Haden pounded on the door. "Claire? Claire?"

"Hold on a minute." He could hear the slap of her bare feet on the wood as she came towards the door.

He stood poised as the chain was removed, and the bolt turned.

When she opened the inside door, she stood there dressed in a pair of short- shorts and an extra-long t-shirt that had a teddy bear in glasses on it, reading a book. It read 'Wild Book Lover. Beware.' Her wet hair hung in dark brown ringlets around her shoulders. She held a bloody tissue in her hand.

Haden's mouth went dry. The palms of his hands began to sweat, so he placed them both on the pint of ice cream. He shook his head. How could any woman look so appealing while holding a bloody wad of tissue?

"Sorry, I wasn't expecting anyone. I'd just stepped out of the shower when I heard you knock."

"How'd you get the bloody toe?"

"Oh," said Claire as she bent to look at it, causing the teddy bear on her shirt to wiggle. "I jammed my toe on the hope chest at the end of my bed. That's where my clothes were."

Haden tensed. He wasn't going to touch that comment with a million-foot pole.

"Lord, help me." He said, repeating his earlier prayer but for a very different reason.

Claire stood up, with a confused look on her face.

Haden didn't wait to be invited in. He reached out and opened the screen door. He had come to comfort her in her time of distress, and she was getting comforted whether she wanted it or not.

Claire moved out of his way and closed the door behind him.

"Henry's not home. He's at Davis's house."

Haden wasn't sure what this was supposed to explain, so he grunted his understanding. "Do you have any antibiotic cream for that toe and a band aid?"

"In the bathroom."

"I'll go get them. You go sit on the couch and apply some pressure. It looks like it's about to drip on the carpet."

Claire leaned over again with the tissue to catch the drops of blood.

Haden groaned, willing himself to turn toward the bathroom and away from Claire in those short shorts.

"Did you really bring ice cream?"

"I did. I got Death by Triple Chocolate. It sounded like the right thing for combating bad news."

"It does sound perfect."

When he returned, she had settled on the far end of the couch with one leg stretched out and the other bent with her foot in her lap, holding her toe.

"I went ahead and put the ice cream in the freezer."

"That's fine."

"Here," Haden sat beside her and grabbed her injured foot. He laid it on his lap and held a fresh paper towel against the toe. "So, Henry's at a friend's house."

"Yeah, I needed some time to pull myself together before I explain to him what's going to happen."

"How about you explain it to me first. Practice." Haden applied the antibiotic cream and wrapped the toe with two bandages, so they wouldn't fall off. But he didn't relinquish his hold on her foot. Instead, he began to rub it.

Claire moaned and placed her other foot in his lap as well. Haden saw the tension begin to drain from her face. As she relaxed, she slid down on the couch and laid her head on the arm rest with her eyes closed.

"So, tell me what you're going to tell Henry."

"Umm. This feels good."

He struggled to keep his hands contained to her feet. Her shapely legs invited his touch, but he needed to move slow if he wanted her trust. "I don't think you're going to tell him that."

∞

Claire opened her eyes to find Haden's dimples spread across his handsome face.

How long had it been since a man had pampered her like this? Too long. She let herself go limp and sighed.

Haden rubbed, putting pressure on the soles of her feet. His strength came through as he worked in circular motions, gentle but firm. That summed up Haden Sawyer.

She watched him. This man with broad shoulders and brown eyes with his curly mop of hair, sitting too close. This was too much, but she couldn't bring herself to move away or demand he stop. Because it had been too long, and it was too good.

"I need to tell him about the Upper and Lower G.I. scopes. There could be other tests, but I know for certain about those."

"How do you think he'll take it? I mean does it upset him with all he's been through, transfusions and everything else?" Haden moved from rubbing one foot to the other.

"You would think it might, but it doesn't. He's so use to it being a part of his life. It's like telling most kids they have to brush their teeth. It's his normal." Claire closed her eyes again. She had to. The feel of Haden's hands moving over her feet and teasing her as he moved up towards her calves made her melt.

"I guess I can see that, but I know it's not easy for you. You know better."

"Yes, I do." Claire soaked in the sensation of his touch and allowed her heart to get lost in it. "There is one good thing that Henry will enjoy. He gets to ride a battery-operated kid size car back to the room where they do the tests."

"He'll love that. Will they put him to sleep?"

"I don't know, but they'll need him to be still."

"Henry will love the car. Any boy would."

"Well, you know how truck crazy he is. He'll have a heyday with one he can drive." When Claire looked up, Haden's eyes were trained on her face. They fell into silence as Haden drew circles on her ankles with his thumbs.

Claire sat up and took Haden's hand. "Thank you. That was wonderful."

Haden cleared his throat. "No, problem. What do you say to some ice cream?"

"That sounds good. I'll get the bowls." Claire got up to go to the kitchen, thinking she'd bring a bowl back to him, but Haden followed her.

"I have something I need to tell you."

Claire was pulling the ice cream from the freezer and stopped, mid action. Turning, she said, "Not more bad news. I can't handle any more." She took a step forward and slammed the freezer door shut.

It was as if something erupted inside her. She spewed. "I mean, I've heard from the doctor, more tests when I was hoping for remission. Ryan calls, out of the blue. I don't even know how he got my cell phone number." Claire flung open the drawer where the spoons were located and jerked out two. "It's been two phones ago since he had my number. Do you know he had the nerve to ask to speak to Henry? What's that about? Right?"

Haden leaned his shoulder against the door jamb and watched.

"He hasn't spoken to Henry since he was three... years... old." Claire stabbed the spoons in the air with each word as if she were dotting an exclamation mark. "The nerve!"

"You've already said that."

Claire ignored him. She grabbed the ice cream scoop out of the bowl on her counter that held odds and ends of utensils.

She ripped the lid off the ice cream, digging the scoop hard into the frosty mass, muttering.

She hadn't heard Haden come up behind her. He touched her hand that was holding the scoop and took it from her. "I think I better do this if it's going to make it into the bowls."

Claire relented. "Okay, but you'd better give me a King Kong sized portion." Claire sat in one of the stools at her counter and watched Haden, making sure he did as he was told.

"So, Ryan called you. That's interesting."

Claire noticed the steel in Haden's voice. "Yeah, I couldn't believe it."

Haden pushed a bowl of Death by Triple Chocolate towards Claire. She took a bite. "Umm...perfect." She let her voice rumble over the word. "You know you have the makings of a great girlfriend. You come over when I need to vent. You rub my feet to relieve tension, and you bring ice cream. Those are pretty much the requirements of a best girlfriend. You nailed it."

"Gee, thanks." Haden scooped a bite and licked the spoon. The action mesmerized her. She looked down into her own bowl when he caught her staring.

"But that's not what I want to be for you. That's what I wanted to tell you, I talked to my mom. I told her the truth about us."

Claire's heart skipped a beat. "That there is no us." She stabbed her ice cream with her spoon.

"Yes. No, No," He frowned at her. "I told her that us being together started out as a lie, but even she can see how much I care for you."

"Haden, as I have demonstrated here today, I'm a mess. My life is full of messiness. It entails doctors and laundry and kid's toys. Don't even get me started on the mounds of bills I'm trying to tame. No one needs that. You have Sarah. She still cares for you, and I think part of the reason she returned to Miller Creek is to win you back. It's obvious she's had second thoughts about calling off the wedding."

Claire could've sworn she saw a spark of panic in Haden's eyes, but whatever it was passed in a snap.

"I don't think Sarah's here to win me back. She got a great job opportunity. That's all." Haden faced Claire leaning his elbows on the counter. "Look, let me take you to the baseball game Friday night. It'll be a real date with nothing in the way." As he said this, he reached out and took her hand in his and began kissing her fingers. His cold lips against her warm skin sent chills of varying types over her body.

Then he intertwined his fingers with hers. "It'll take yours and Henry's mind off of Wednesday's tests for a little while. Besides, Henry will love watching the Little League players run rings around Kyle."

Claire knew the answer had to be no. She had no room in her life for anyone other than Henry. If only Haden would stop nibbling the inside of her wrist, she might be able to form the word.

∞

Haden slammed his hand against the steering wheel as he drove towards his house. Irritation and guilt boiled together inside of him. He had spent the evening with Claire until around seven when she needed to go pick up Henry. The opportunity to tell her about Sarah and the wedding had presented itself like a neon sign flashing at him. Do it now; do it now.

But he had chickened out. Haden groaned.

With the warm breeze blowing through the rolled down windows, he replayed the conversation in his head. Why had he hesitated? But he knew why.

Fear.

He couldn't lose her; she was just starting to open up. She had agreed to go with him Friday night, but she had her doubts about him because of the lie he'd told his mom.

What would she think if she knew he had been the one to call off the wedding but let Sarah take the blame. She'd think he was a louse, and for good reason. He had taken the easy way out because of his pride and broken heart.

He eyed the Bible sitting on the seat. He should've told her. He hadn't meant to deceive anyone. Everyone made assumption, and then it took on a life of its own. But not telling her tonight, that was all on him.

He pulled up into his short drive and turned off the engine. The warmth of the evening settled over him as he sat listening to the sounds of twilight. His heart torn between what was right and what he wanted. How was he ever going to straighten out a whole town's misconception and still keep the woman he loved?

Chapter Twenty-two

Adele entered Betty's kitchen, shutting the back door behind her.

"It's me, Betty." She slid the bags of groceries onto the island, tossing her purse beside them.

"I'm in here." Betty's voice flowed from the office.

Adele found Betty stretched out on the love seat. "I put the groceries in the kitchen on my way in." She took a seat in the chair. "Boy, was the supermarket busy. I'd forgotten how many people shop on Fridays." Adele slipped off her shoes and wiggled her toes.

"Thanks for doing that for me." Betty smiled.

"No, problem. Glad to help."

"You'd think since they let me go I'd be able to do my normal activities, but these days, once you poop, you're out of there. They don't let you lay around and enjoy being out of commission." Betty shook her head, grinning.

It pleased Adele to see her sister-in-law doing so well. She had worried she might fall into the blues now that she was alone and stuck at home for the next few weeks. She didn't even want to think about the chemo and radiation treatments to come.

But, she should've known better. Betty's sense of humor gave her an advantage over other people. She could find the good in even the hardest of times. It was her sense of humor and her silver lining outlook that had kept her and Adele pieced together during Otis's illness.

"Have you heard from the boys?" Adele slumped in the chair like a teenager.

"Kyle came by with flowers. He's so thoughtful for one so young."

"Well, he views you as his second mom. You put up with enough of his shenanigans as a boy. You've earned the title. Were they the ones on the counter with all the daisies?" Adele asked, lifting her eyebrows.

"Yeah, it appears he was distracted when he picked them out."

"Umm. Daisies seem to be on his mind a lot these days."

"Yes, they do." Both women laughed. Betty held a pillow to her chest and winced. "I also heard from Jed and Haden. Jed texted since he was out at the Henderson site, and Haden called."

"It's nice to know we raised 'em right."

Betty rolling onto her side, leaned up on her elbow. "Speaking of distracted, did I mention to you that Haden fessed up about his relationship with Claire?" A twinkle appeared in her eye.

"No, you did not!" Adele popped up straight in her chair. "When did this happen?"

"Right after the surgery. He couldn't wait. It was eating at him."

"Yeah, Kyle said he's been grouchy the last few weeks at work, and yet, happier in a miserable sort of way."

"It's like sweet and sour sauce." Betty supplied.

"Exactly. So, he came clean about the lie. Good for him. Now, he can pursue her without anything in the way."

"Well almost." Betty frowned. "He told me something else that he needs to get straightened out, or it could interfere with our happy ever after ending."

"What's that?" Adele asked.

"Sarah's not the one who called off the wedding, he is."

"Get out of town! I could've sworn Haden told me himself that she'd called it off." Adele leaned back, running her conversations with Haden about this subject through her mind. No, to her recollection, he never did say those exact words. He hadn't commented one way or the other.

"He said he let everyone make their own assumptions. Since she left town soon after, everyone thought she had been the one to call it off. So, he didn't correct them." Betty's smile engulfed her face and flowed into her eyes.

"What now?" Adele asked aware of her sister-in-law's fluctuating emotions. She wondered if the medications were causing this ebb and flow.

"I was thinking about that silly-in-love grin Haden wears every time he's near Claire. It reminds me of how Otis looked at me when we were young and first dating. He cares for her. That he did say."

Adele's heart swelled. "Oooh, good. Matchmaking works so much better when everybody involved cooperates." Then she added, "But you said this could interfere with our plans. How?"

"Claire."

"I'm going to need more than that to go on. What about Claire?"

"Adele, you told me yourself she's scared to give her heart to anyone. Her ex-husband abandoned her when she needed him most. There's no way she'll get involved with a man if she thinks he'll leave. No way." Betty shook her head against the pillow.

"Oh, you're right." Adele sighed, leaning her head back against the chair. "All this work, being a fairy godmother, encouraging the two of them along.

"It can't end with both Haden and Claire losing out." She said to Betty who had rolled over on to her back. "They've been so good for each other. That's got to mean something." Adele sounded desperate.

"It does. We need to pull out the big guns."

"Yes, you're right. We should've pulled them out earlier, but I'm a slow learner." Adele stood and moved to the loveseat as Betty scooted over.

"Me too, but it's never too late to pray."

Adele sat down, took Betty's hands and began. *"Dear Lord…."*

∞

Haden left Henry standing by the fence watching the Little League players warm up. He picked three seats on the third row, so it would be easy for Henry and Claire to get up and down. No need to add extra stairs, though Henry seemed to be having a high energy day.

Haden watched Henry wave to Kyle who ran over to them. "Hey, I'm so glad you could come to the game."

"Mom said your team is a bunch of birds, but I don't see no birds." Henry frowned.

Kyle grinned and looked up at Claire who sat next to Haden on the third row of the bleachers. "Thanks a lot there, Claire."

She returned his grin. "My pleasure."

"My team is the Yellow Hammers which is the Alabama state bird. I'm sure that's what your mom meant."

"Oh, so no birds?"

Kyle reached over the chain link fence to rumple the little boy's hair. "No birds, pal. Sorry. But here's a pom-pom to use." He handed him the yellow pom-pom that shed the minute Henry shook it. "Cheer loud, okay?"

"I will."

Kyle ran back to his dugout, and Haden stood to help Henry up the steps. He sat him between himself and Claire. It seemed right the three of them here, cheering for the team his company sponsored. "Go Yellow!" Henry stood and shook the pom-pom; yellow streamers fell all over. "Go Yellow!"

"He's excited. This is his first live baseball game." The smile Claire flashed electrified him. Her vivid green eyes danced as they followed the young players out on the field. "Aren't they adorable?"

"Yes, they're something else, all right." Haden didn't take his eyes off Claire. She wore jeans and a soft blue peasant's blouse that screamed feminine appeal to him. If he had his way, he'd pull her close.

She turned and caught him staring. He loved the way she blushed.

"I appreciate you meeting me here."

"That's okay. I know you've been working late, trying to catch up from being out earlier this week. I didn't mind. I'm glad you asked me." She corrected, "us to come tonight."

"Not as glad as I am that you guys agreed to come, on a date…" Haden reached over and took her hand. "a real date with me." She nudged him with her shoulder as Henry chanted, "Go Hammers, Go Yellow."

After the National Anthem played, a teenaged boy walked up the bleachers past Henry carrying a hotdog.

"Hey, can I have a hot dog?" Henry propped his elbows on Haden's leg and leaned up towards his face. "Please."

Haden glanced over at Claire who nodded. "Sure, buddy, you want to go with me? You can help me tote the drinks back."

"Yeah, I'm hungry," As Haden stood, Henry grabbed his hand. Haden's heart lightened.

By the time they returned from the concession stand, the inning was under way. The Yellow Hammers were at bat, but the way things were going, it looked like they were about to strike out.

Claire helped Henry with his drink as he climbed back to their spot on the third row. Once seated, Haden handed Claire her drink and hot dog while he got himself situated to watch the game.

As he bit into the warm bun, he heard his name buzz in his ear. "Haden, I thought that was you."

Choking down the hot dog, he answered, "Hi, Sarah, what are you doing here?"

"Oh, I had a little down time, so I thought I'd come root for the Yellow Hammers."

"You were never interested in baseball when we dated. As I recall, you hated it when I dragged you to the ball field."

"Well, it's a small town. Not much to do." Sarah sat down next to him on his left.

Claire sat frowning on his right.

Trapped.

Chapter Twenty-three

"I thought I'd have to sit alone. Good thing you're here." Sarah leaned into his shoulder and nudged him just like Claire had. This did not escape her notice.

"Well, I'm here with Claire and Henry. You remember Claire."

"Yes, I remember." Sarah glanced over at Claire and Henry but made no attempt at conversation. "I don't mind if they sit with us." With that, Sarah wrapped her arm through Haden's and snuggled closer.

Haden furrowed his brow.

Claire ate her hot dog in two bites, getting ready to make her exit. She wanted to leave, but she figured that's what Sarah wanted, to be alone with Haden. So, assessing her situation, she stayed, not giving Sarah the satisfaction of running her off.

"You know, Sarah, I've heard a lot of good things about the architecture firm you're working for. Are you enjoying your new job?" Claire moved closer to Haden and leaned around him pressing her hand on his shoulder for support.

"Yes, I am." Sarah answered, also moving closer to Haden and leaning her arm on his thigh.

Claire bit her bottom lip as she watched her.

"But the thing I love most about being back in Miller Creek besides reconnecting with everyone, is being able to live in the apartment above the empty flower shop on Main Street."

"Oh, does it hold special meaning for you?" Claire sat poised moving her hand to Haden's leg. He raised an eyebrow

"Go Kyle, Go Yellow." Henry yelled, only stopping long enough to take another bite of his hot dog.

"Don't jump with your mouth full. You might choke." Claire moved back to her own seat. Henry reminded her of her first duty, that of mother. Shame washed over her. Every time she encountered Sarah her emotions got the best of her. She did the craziest things when it came to this woman.

"Okay, Mommy." Henry shook his pom-pom, making a swishing noise and dropping more streamers.

Claire turned her attention back to Sarah who had not relinquished an inch of Haden territory. "Yes, the apartment was where Haden proposed."

Claire saw Haden stiffen, his eyes on her. Claire clenched her teeth. "Oh, I see. I guess that would be a special place for the two of you."

"Uh huh, I remember it like it was yesterday." Sarah's voice took on a dreamy quality. "He was doing a remodel job for the owner, and I took him his favorite lunch from Adele's Café, a bacon cheeseburger. Special delivery." She squeezed his leg.

Haden jumped up, spilling his drink down the front of his shirt. He blotted at the stain with a napkin to no avail. "Excuse me." He bolted down the bleachers, heading to the concession stand.

"Haden told me that the two of you were engaged."

"Yes, we were. I hate that things didn't work out for us. I was willing, but Haden didn't think we could get beyond our differences."

Claire knew she shouldn't, but she couldn't help herself. "Do you mind me asking what those differences were?"

Sarah's face glowed with the delight of one who had sprung a trap and caught her prey. "No, not at all. We didn't agree about having children."

Claire's stomach plummeted to her feet. A wave of nausea washed over her. "No wonder you called off the wedding."

"Oh, no. I didn't call off the wedding. It was Haden. Didn't he tell you?"

Claire's head swam. "He called off the wedding? He's the one that bailed?"

"Yes, he didn't want to try to work it out. He gave up on the whole relationship."

Claire's chest tightened. Panic seized her.

She grabbed her purse and started digging for her keys.

"Did I say something to upset you?" Sarah asked with all the right inflections and a hint of innocence.

Claire popped up out of her seat. She needed to leave. She needed to think.

This man who she believed she could trust, who had been so gentle and kind with Henry, didn't want children.

"I need to go. I'm not feeling too well. It must've been the hotdog." Claire touched Henry's shoulder to get his attention. "It's time for us to go home."

"But Mommy, the game isn't over, and I haven't finished my drink." Henry pulled away from Claire's touch.

"You can bring it with us."

"No, I can't. You don't let me drink soda in the car. You said it makes it sticky."

"This one time, you can." Claire picked up the cup and the empty wrappers.

Haden came back down the baseline and up the bleachers. "Where are you going?" Claire didn't answer but continued to gather the trash.

"Here, let me help you."

"You've helped enough," she jerked her hand away from his and swallowed back the hot tears.

"What's that supposed to mean?" He looked at Sarah, who shrugged her shoulders but didn't say a word.

Claire stood straight. "It means, Haden Sawyer, I have a kid. One that I love. I'm a complete package. Henry doesn't go away if someone else comes into my life. He will always, always be my number one priority."

"I know that." Haden's mouth flattened into a straight line as his jaw tensed. "I don't understand. What's going on here?"

"I almost made the same mistake." Claire shook her head. "You'd think I'd learn. You said you wanted to be there for me and Henry, and I believed you." Now, Claire looked him in the eye. "But why shouldn't that be a lie too."

Haden didn't move.

Claire made her way down the bleachers, taking Henry's hand and helping him down. "I'm leaving. If you still want to know what's going on, ask Sarah. I'm sure she'll be thrilled to tell you."

Claire stormed off in the direction of her car. Stopped, turned and marched back. "And don't look for me at the office, tomorrow. I quit."

∞

Haden barreled towards the gravel parking lot, ready to put this disaster of a night behind him. Why was it every time he moved one step forward with Claire, someone knocked him three steps back.

From what Claire had said and the little Sarah had supplied, he could guess what was wrong. He knew the blame lay squarely on his shoulders. He'd had ample time to tell Claire about Sarah and the wedding, but he always talked himself out of it. He kicked the gravel, sending it skittering.

He saw Jed pull in next to his truck and park. A groan escaped his lips.

Jed stepped out of the cab, moving toward Haden. "Was that Claire I saw leaving in that cloud of white dust? What's got her so riled?"

"Go ask Sarah."

"Sarah? Is she here?" Haden saw the tension creep across Jed's face.

"Yeah, she's here, and I'd better leave before I forget I'm a gentleman."

"Don't tell me you've blown it with Claire because of Sarah? I told you to be sure if you were going to pursue a relationship with her. She's not just some woman." Jed flexed his fists that hung at his side.

"Not that it's any of your business, but I'm sure about my feelings for Claire."

"Not from where I stand." Jed pulled himself up to his full height. Haden responded by doing the same. "You can't play around when it comes to her, little brother."

He knew Jed was pushing his buttons. "Who made you the expert on Claire Reed?" Haden took a step closer to Jed.

"Look, you don't have to be a genius to see how much pressure she's under."

"I'm aware of the pressure; I'm aware she has a child; I'm aware how wonderful and perfect she is." Haden hissed.

"Are you sure about that? Because the way she tore out of here, would say otherwise. I thought this was supposed to be a date."

Haden tightened his jaw. "You've been sniffing around Claire like a wolf whose found fresh meat since I hired her."

"As I recall, we hired her."

"Now, I'm telling you back off."

Jed took a step closer to Haden. Haden could smell taco on his breath. "I'll back off after I'm sure your intentions are honorable."

"Like yours?" Haden reached out and pushed him.

"Why, you little runt." Jed charged at Haden, pushing him back against his truck and pinning him there with his arm across his chest. Haden's back screamed from the impact against the metal.

"Are you trying to kill me?" Haden asked as he locked his heel around Jed's calf and pulled his leg out from under him. Jed hit the gravel butt first.

"I can't believe you did that."

"What, defend myself? You started it." Haden said as he rubbed his lower back.

Jed mimicked, "You started it," and broke out into a full belly laugh. "Look at us. We sound like we're twelve, and all because of a woman."

"Yeah, but what a woman." Haden smiled and offered Jed a hand up. Jed eyed him before he took it.

"I can't help caring for Claire." Jed wiped the white dust from his jeans. "She's kind and full of fun, but she's made it clear you're the one she wants."

"I don't know about that. She seems more at ease with you than she ever is with me."

"That's the problem. I don't make her nervous."

Haden nodded his understanding. "I see what you mean."

"I want to know that you're serious about this. I don't want her to get hurt."

"I won't hurt her. I love her."

Jed held his palms up in surrender. "That's all I wanted to hear."

Haden frowned. "Why didn't you start with that. Now, my back will be stiff for a week."

"You're back? My rear feels like it's been kicked by a stubborn mule."

Haden chuckled. "Maybe, just a slightly hard headed one." He looked down at his feet before he continued. "There's one other thing I should mention."

"What's that?" Jed leaned his hip against Haden's truck.

"Claire quit."

∞

The choir sang the last note of Amazing Grace signaling the end of the service. As the congregation closed their hymnals and rose to leave,

Haden tried to squeeze around his Aunt Adele but found he was trapped.

The Ladies of the Helping Hand Society had rushed her. Cornered, she fielded their questions about Betty's surgery. The ladies of the Society wanted to offer their services and to bring meals. These ladies could cook circles around any chef.

Haden sat down. He figured he'd be here awhile. Kyle joined him.

"Is Betty in a lot of pain?" asked Mrs. Styles.

"No, they have her on some strong pain killers. It's amazing what they can do these days. We're just so thankful they were able to get it all. I think that's what frightened me the most." Adele placed her hand over her heart. "I don't know what I'd do without Betty."

"Umm, girl. We're all so glad you don't have to find out. She's been a part of this community, well, since forever," said Mrs. Clark who had been around about the same amount of time.

The ladies fussed over who would bring what on which night, but at last, they got it all planned out. Mrs. Styles, the reigning president of the society, took down the names and dates as the ladies volunteered.

"Now, tell Betty we are all praying for her, and if there are any hiccups with the dinners, have her call me. I'll keep the master list and email the others the schedule."

"Oh, thank you all so much. I know this will mean the world to Betty. With all this fine cuisine, she'll gain back her weight in no time."

"Coming from you Adele, we take that as high praise," said Mrs. Styles.

As the ladies of the society left, Haden turned his attention to his aunt.

“Oh boys, I’m sorry. I didn’t know you were waiting on me. I would’ve hurried.”

“No, you wouldn’t have, Mom. You only have one speed when it comes to people, attentive. You are after all, the hostess of the universe.” Kyle beamed with pride.

“I guess it’s an occupational hazard.” She sat on the pew next to Haden with her Bible in her lap.

Kyle looked at his watch. “I promised Daisey I’d go with her on a picnic. I’m supposed to pick her up in twenty minutes, and it’ll take me that long to go home and change.”

Haden knew what he wanted. “Don’t worry. I’m going over to Mom’s to check in on her. I’ll give my favorite aunt a ride over.”

“Did you hear that?” she looked around Haden at Kyle. “His favorite aunt.”

“Well, you’re my favorite mother, so that beats his out.” Kyle stood and leaned over Haden to kiss his mother’s cheek. “I’ll call you later tonight to see how you’re doing.”

Once in the parking lot, Haden held the door of the truck for his aunt and made sure she was settled before going around to the driver’s side. As he slid in and buckled up, Adele asked, “So how are things going with Claire?”

He clenched his hands around the steering wheel. He had spent the majority of the morning trying to think about anything else. Now, his Aunt was forcing him to think about the one subject he was avoiding.

“Not great.” His jaw tensed at the thought of Friday night.

Adele turned in her seat to face him. “What happened?”

Haden leaned back against the seat. "For starters, I told Mom that Claire and I weren't dating. That I had lied about the whole thing because of Sarah."

"I know that already, but that doesn't tell me what happened between you and Claire. I thought she'd be relieved that you came clean with your mom."

"She was."

"But…" supplied Adele.

"But Sarah showed up at the little league baseball game where I had taken Claire and Henry. It was supposed to be our first real date." Haden frowned creating creases in his brow.

"Everything was going along fine, then Sarah showed up, and she hung on this arm," Haden lifted his left hand. "Then Claire situated herself, leaning on my leg." He patted his right thigh. "Then before I knew it I was wearing my drink down the front of my shirt.

"I excused myself, glad to get out from between them, to be honest. But when I returned, Claire yelled at me that she was a complete package, kid and all, and then quit her job."

Adele grinned and shook her head. "Oh no, I'm sorry Haden." She patted his hand. "Did you find out what was bothering her?

"No, but I have some idea of what Sarah told her."

"What could Sarah tell her that you haven't?" Adele asked.

Haden groaned and flopped his head against the seat. "Plenty."

"Oh Haden, what did you keep from her?"

"From the little I got from Sarah, because believe me she wasn't cooperative, Claire knows I was the one who called off the wedding."

"Your mother told me about that."

"Of course, she did." Haden put the key in the ignition and started the engine.

After revving it, he threw the gear shift into reverse and pulled out of the parking space, missing the car behind him by inches.

"I'd like to arrive in one piece, please."

"Sorry, Aunt Adele." Haden worked his jaw muscle; his mind racing from one point to another. "How did this get so messed up?"

"Lies. Plain and simple."

Haden huffed. "You're right. I should've told everyone the truth about me and Sarah from the beginning and not let them jump to conclusions. I guess I took the easy way out."

"That's what Claire's afraid of now. That you'll take the easy way out like her ex-husband. You have to remember she's been struggling on her own for some time."

Haden shot her a look. He knew she was right. It was like Jed said, she needed to know he'd be there, rock solid, no matter what.

"You know Claire reminds me a little of myself when your Uncle Lars died overseas. It was your Dad and Mom who took me in. They showed me I was stronger with family than without. I had Kyle, and like Claire, I came with an add on."

"What should I do? Got any advice for me?"

"As a matter of fact, I do. Go tell her the truth. All of it. Start at the beginning and don't stop until you reach this moment. After that, and this is the important part, be there for her and for Henry. It's going to take showing, not telling, if you want Claire to believe you care for her."

Haden absorbed this deep into his heart. He knew his aunt was right. But how? What would convince Claire that he wanted, no needed, her and Henry in his life?

∞

It felt weird being home all day, and even weirder not seeing Haden.

Claire spent the day trekking back and forth between being angry with him and being angry with herself.

She shouldn't have quit.

He shouldn't have lied.

She shouldn't have gone along with his charades.

He shouldn't have asked her to.

Her big accomplishment today: a whopper of a headache.

Claire made something easy for supper, unable to focus on anything too complicated. She sat across from Henry who was twirling his fork in his spaghetti. It took everything she had not to reach over and do it for him.

She turned to her computer which sat on the table and combed through the job sites, trying to find something she could start soon. She had even looked over the local paper she had picked up from the grocery. The work forecast in Miller Creek looked gloomy and overcast.

Her rent would come due in a week. The monthly payments to the doctors, hospital, and daycare added up quick. She couldn't afford to lose her spot at Mrs. Nolen's. It had taken too long to get accepted, and she needed a safe place for Henry after Kindergarten let out at noon.

Henry caught Claire's attention as he pulled himself up onto his knees to reach his drink.

He had been quiet throughout the meal. "So, how was school today?"

"Mrs. Cooper said we could play on the playground tomorrow if everything dries." He took a sip from his cup.

"Well, that'll be fun." She dipped her French bread into the sauce.

"I like to play outside because I can watch for the big trucks."

Claire braced herself; she knew what was coming. He had asked the same thing every day for the last week.

"When will Haden take me to see the big trucks?" Henry succeeded in capturing a few noodles onto his fork. He caught the strays that stuck out with his tongue as he slurped the mass off the utensil. A trail of sauce appeared on his chin.

Claire swallowed the lump in her own throat. "Honey, I've told you. We might not see much of Haden anymore. Mommy doesn't work for him. I've got to look for a new job."

"But he promised. Haden said he would take me to see them."

"Well, he said a lot of things most of which weren't…" she stopped herself.

"Weren't what, Mommy?"

"Never mind. Eat your supper and let me do a little more work." She turned her attention back to the computer.

"I thought you said you needed a new job. How can you be working?" Henry tilted his head, giving Claire a perplexed look.

She sighed, the headache getting the better of her. She rubbed her temples and closed her eyes, trying to find relief. "I'm working on finding work."

"That sounds weird."

"Yes, it does, doesn't it?" Claire opened one eye to see Henry back to twirling his noodles onto his fork.

Seeing Henry occupied, she went back to her search. She didn't get very far before he interrupted, again. "Mom, do you think Haden will take us to another baseball game? I want to go."

Frowning, she said, "I don't think so."

"Shoot a monkey!" Claire grinned at his use of her own expression. "I wanted another hotdog. It was good."

"Well, eat your dinner. It's good too." He stuck his bottom lip out but stabbed a meatball and bit into it with gusto.

Leaving Haden behind was going to be hard. He and Henry had begun without needing a beginning; they had started as if they had always been a part of one another's life, natural. Now, because of her quick temper, she had brought about the end.

Henry cleared his plate from the table and went to take his bath while she cleaned up the kitchen. Her hands in the soapy water made her think of the Sunday at Betty's house. The good food, noise and laughter, Daisey coloring with Henry, and the way Haden had lifted Henry up to see the pies. Family, she ached for it.

As she swished the suds over one of the plates, her mind drifted further, to the first time Haden had kissed her in the office. If the desk hadn't been between them, she might have let it go on and on. But it's cold hard surface had broken the spell.

She turned the faucet on to rise the plate.

Ryan was a good kisser, but Haden's kisses sizzled. She

remembered the feel of him kissing her wrist when he asked her out to the ball game. She shivered.

"Mom, Mom…MOM," Claire jerked. "The waters running over in the bath tub."

Claire pushed the faucet off and ran to the bathroom. "Oh no," She waded through the water, getting the hems of her jeans soaked. Turning off the water, she reached in and unplugged the tub. "Grab a towel."

Henry obeyed and reached for the towels stacked on the shelving unit behind the toilet. Claire began shaking them out and throwing them onto the floor. With each addition, the water began to disappear.

"Go get a laundry basket from the utility room."

"Please," corrected Henry.

"Please," said Claire, suppressing a groan.

Henry took off like a shot, reappearing moments later with a basket.

Claire swiped a towel across the floor. Once soaked, she held it above the tub to wring it out. One by one, she repeated the steps until all the towels had been wrung and put into the laundry basket. Henry set off down the hall, trying to drag the basket behind him, determined to do his part. Claire pushed from behind.

When they entered the kitchen, she heard her phone ringing from the depths of her purse. Digging it out, she checked the screen. The caller's name and photo glared back at her, Haden Sawyer.

Henry stood next to her with the basket of towels. "Oh, it's Haden. Mom answer it."

"No,"

"Why not? He might want to invite us to the game. You've got to answer." Henry's voice rose with excitement.

"I'm not answering. Now, let's put the basket in the utility room, so I can start a load of towels." Claire sent the call to voice mail.

Henry's face fell, but he grabbed the handle and started dragging the basket as she pushed. They took it to the small room off the kitchen where the laundry machines lived.

After she started a load of towels, she checked her phone to see if he had left a message. He had left not one message but seven.

Persistent. She laid her phone back on the kitchen table by her computer.

"Let's go get your bath ready."

Henry followed her down the hall and this time, Claire waited as the tub filled. "Can I get my dinosaurs to play with?"

"Sure, go get them." While she waited, she fished around in the medicine cabinet and found the aspirin and downed two.

Once Henry was in the tub, she meandered back into the kitchen to finish the dishes. Her phone rang. She ignored it.

What if it's about Betty? If I don't answer and its important, I'll feel like a heel. Claire bit her lip and plunged her hands deeper into the water. The phone quieted. Her shoulders relaxed.

A minute later, it rang again. She groaned. Thoughts of work flooded into her mind.

What if it's about the contract for the Wymore site? It'd be horrible if Haden loses that bid because of me. It's going to mean a big payday for Sawyer Construction.

The ringing persisted until she pulled the red dish towel from the hanger to dry her hands; then it stopped.

She finished and tossed the towel onto the counter. Claire silenced the phone.

Returning to the sink, she set her mind to the task of scraping the hardened noodles from the Dutch oven.

If it rings again, I'm ignoring it. I won't answer. She grabbed the scrubber and applied elbow grease to the dried-on food.

The buzz of the phone broke the silence. It vibrated, scooting along the table surface until it teetered on the edge.

Annoyed, she dried her hands and answered.

"What?"

Chapter Twenty-four

Haden hesitated. This was a bad idea.

"What do you want?" Claire sounded irked.

She had every right to be, he thought. "I'm standing on your front porch. Let me in."

Haden caught Claire peeking out the living room blinds. There he stood, one hand holding his phone, the other holding a colorful bouquet of spring flowers. Exposed.

"Can I come in? Please?" Haden looked directly at Claire. He saw the blinds pop back into place and heard the patter of her bare feet hitting the wood floor.

"I don't want to talk to you." She said into the phone, but he could hear her through the door as well.

"Look, Claire. I'm not here just to see you. I came to keep a promise to Henry." He leaned against the door jamb.

"What promise is that?" She sounded less angry, more curious, so he seized the moment.

"The one about the big trucks. That kid of yours is nuts about trucks. I have to keep my promise. I can't disappoint him. I know you think I'm a louse. And I might be, but not for the reasons you think. I'd like the chance to change that opinion."

"You are a louse. Anyone who doesn't like kids."

"Claire, have I ever given you a reason to think that I didn't like

Henry?"

"No, but…"

"I don't know what happened at the game, but at least give me a chance to explain. Hear my side before you make any decisions… about me or quitting."

There was no answer, but he heard the click of the lock.

He hung up the phone and tucked it into his back pocket.

"Come in," she said, but stopped short of opening the screen door. Her hand went straight to her mouth as her eyes grew wide.

She pushed open the screen door and stepped out onto the porch. "You brought a dump truck."

"And flowers," Haden handed her the bouquet. Claire lifted it to her nose and closed her eyes, inhaling. It pleased Haden that Claire enjoyed his peace offering.

"They're lovely."

"I hope Henry likes the truck as much as you do."

"Henry!" Claire bolted for the door. "He's in the bath tub. I shouldn't have left him alone."

Haden followed close on her heels. He stood in the hallway as she knocked on the door. "Henry, are you okay in there?'

"Yeah, the dinosaurs are taking over the world."

"Again?" she called.

Haden relaxed. He had gotten further than he had hoped.

"Guess who's here?"

"Umm, I don't know. Who?"

"Haden, and he brought you a surprise."

They heard the water start to drain, some clunking around that could've been toys being thrown into a container, and then feet slapping on the tile floor like he was jumping up and down. "I'm coming. I'm coming."

A minute later, a wet Henry emerged from the bathroom with pajama's sticking to his skin and his hair poking out all over his head. "What kind of surprise? I love surprises."

"I can see that," said Haden. "Do you have any slippers?"

"Yeah, I got slippers."

"Go, put them on, and I'll take you to see your surprise."

"Awesome." And down the hall he ran, swinging himself around the door post into his room. Before Haden could explain anything to Claire, Henry was back, grabbing Haden's hand. "Okay, ready."

Haden let out a chuckle. "Okay, let's go. Mom, you'll need your shoes too."

"Why?"

"Can you play along?"

Claire frowned but went to her room for her shoes.

When she returned, she found Haden holding Henry. The burst of energy taking its toll.

"Let me put the flowers in some water."

Henry let out a groan. "Hurry, Mommy."

Once back, she placed the vase of flowers on the entry table.

"Okay, buddy. Let's go."

Henry let out a yell the moment he laid eyes on the dump truck. "Can I keep it?" Henry asked in awe.

"No, afraid not Super Henry, but if Mom says yes, we can all go for a ride in it. You can sit in my lap and help me drive."

"Is that legal?" Claire asked, crossing her arms.

"I'm going to head over to the Wymore site. Right now, there's plenty of room for a little driving lesson, and everyone should be cleared out by this time on a Monday evening. So, it should be safe."

"Alright, I guess."

"Y-e-s-s-s" said Henry pumping his arms in the air.

∞

Wednesday morning, the hospital hallway teemed with people. Claire walked beside Henry as he drove the child size truck through the hall on their way to the children's waiting room. Henry blew the horn as he passed the nurses.

How fitting after the other night with Haden. The evening had been special for Henry.

For her, it had been strained and awkward. Keeping her distance from Haden, was hard. She wanted to throw her arms around his neck and squeeze him for being so sweet and keeping his promise about the truck. But her fears wouldn't let her. He had left one woman over kids, what was different now.

When Haden had taken them home, Henry held his hand and hers as they walked to the door like a family. He asked Haden to stay and tuck him into bed. Haden had declined, and the disappointment covered her little boy's face.

Her heart ached for Henry now. He had grown attached to Haden. She guessed he was trying to fill that void in his life. Even at five, he knew something was missing. Every little boy needed a father. She watched

Henry do figure eights in the children's waiting room.

"Hey, I brought you coffee. Two sugars and some creamer, right?"

Startled by the closeness of the voice, Claire turned to find Haden holding a cup of coffee and a baseball glove. "What are you doing here?"

"I'm not letting you go through this alone. Here have some coffee."

Claire took the cup from his hand. The aroma wafted around her. Taking a sip, she let the tension roll from her shoulders. Here was Haden again. He was like a stray dog she couldn't get rid of and maybe didn't want to. "Thanks for coming. I could use the company."

"Haden, look at me." Henry honked the horn.

Haden walked over and inspected the truck. Henry's teddy bear, Baby, sat in the passenger seat. "Wow, that's awesome."

"I know. Look I can drive with no hands." The boy took off again.

"I wouldn't do that. You're such a good driver. You'd hate to have a wreck and ruin your record. Besides, you've got real road experience."

"I sure do. I'm a real truck driver." Henry pulled up to Haden. "Is that for me?" He asked pointing to the baseball glove.

"Yes, it is." Haden squatted and handed him the glove.

Henry inspected it. "Why'd you bring me a baseball glove?" he asked.

"Because you're being so brave. I thought you deserved a reward."

"I am?" Henry scrunched up his face. "How?"

"You're doing something that you've never done before and that takes courage. So, you're being brave."

Henry leaned close to Haden. "I'm not brave. Mom told me all about the machine and the sleep juice, but" Henry whispered, "Baby and I are scared."

A lump rose in Claire's throat as she pushed down the tears.

Haden put his hand on the boy's back. "Brave doesn't mean you're not scared. It means you do what you need to do anyway."

Henry threw his arms around Haden's neck and quick, pulled away. He tucked the ball glove in the seat beside him. "Got to go." He hit the gas pedal and zig-zagged past Haden and his mom.

Haden stood and gestured towards the chairs. "Want to sit?" She nodded, not wanting to risk crying if she spoke.

The two seats that were open sat side-by-side. She had no choice but to sit next to him which was too close for her comfort. She wiggled, leaning her back against the arm, to put some distance between them. Her purse in her lap became a protective barrier.

If I'm going to move on, I need to keep this at the friend level.

"Henry Reed," called the nurse. "We're ready for you."

Henry drove his motorized truck to the doorway. "Wave good-bye to Mom and Dad." Claire tensed.

"Bye, Mom. Bye, Haden." Henry jolted forward in the truck but stopped. "You will be here when I come back?" He directed his question to Haden. His face serious and drawn.

"Yes, I'll be here." He looked at Claire. "I'm not going anywhere."

"Good." Henry hit the gas pedal and followed the nurse in the blue lab coat.

∞

Haden knew it was his moment to do what he needed to do. Scared didn't begin to describe all the emotions he had battled over the last several days. His discovery of how attached he had grown to Claire and Henry in such a short amount of time rattled him. His mind worked hard to convince him that love wasn't possible, not yet, but his heart drove the point home over and over again.

He had wanted to talk to Claire last night about his new discoveries, but she had sent a clear signal that she didn't want to hear what he had to say. So, he had focused on the surprise for Henry and had left the wall between them untouched.

Now or never. "Claire, there is something we need to get cleared up."

"No, everything's fine. You don't have to explain yourself to me." Claire lifted her hand and waved, dismissing his words.

"That's not true. I dragged you into the middle of something that I should've handled, but…" Haden leaned back in his chair and wiped his sweaty hands on his jeans. "was too afraid to meet head on."

"You don't have to do this." Claire fidgeted in her chair.

"I need for you to understand. When Sarah left town, I let everyone think she had called off the wedding. It seemed easier at the time. I didn't relish the thought of rehashing the story with every wedding gift I returned, which she left for me to do. I guess I deserved it though."

"I know you called off the wedding and let others think it was her. Sarah told me. It's no big deal. We all do things that we regret later." Claire hugged her purse in her lap.

"It seemed like a big deal the other night at the baseball game when you stormed off." Haden studied Claire, trying to read her thoughts. His heart pounded.

"Yeah, I admit, I over reacted." Claire wouldn't look him in the eye.

"That's what surprised me. That you would quit your job over that."

She began to play with her purse strap. "It wasn't just that."

"Then what was it?"

Claire hesitated.

"Look, Claire, I can't make this right if I don't know what's going on. Help me out here. You mentioned something about me not liking kids last night at your house. What gave you that idea? Did I do something wrong with Henry that you didn't like?"

"No, no, you've been great with Henry. Better than great."

"Then why on earth would you think that I don't like kids?"

Claire fussed with the straps of her purse, twisting them around her finger. Haden saw the struggle play out on her face.

He leaned close and whispered, "Come on. Tell me, please."

"Alright, if you want to know, but I feel like I'm prying into your business."

"Go on. I want to know."

"Sarah implied that the break up was over having children."

"Yes, it was, but that shouldn't affect our relationship."

"What are you saying. Of course, it's going to affect our relationship real, fake, or otherwise." Claire's voice rose with heat. Haden glanced around to see if they had attracted any attention in the overcrowded room. One lady in her thirties met his gaze with a look of distain.

"Why does this stir you up so bad? The fact that I called off the wedding because she didn't want to have kids, shouldn't be an issue. You already have a kid. Don't you want to have more?" Haden snapped.

Chapter Twenty-five

"Of course, I want more, but the way she told it, you didn't want any, but she did." Claire scooted to the edge of her seat, so she could look Haden straight in the face.

His eyes locked with hers. "That's not true. I wanted kids and thought once we were married she might change her mind, but she started talking about the job offer in Chicago. It became clear we weren't right for each other. I had mistaken compassion and friendship for love.

"To tell the truth, the whole thing goes miles deeper than the difference about whether to have kids or not. Her ambition drives her. She wants money, prestige, recognition, and I want family. Our goals didn't line up."

"Why didn't you see that earlier before you proposed?" Claire asked.

Leaning back in his chair, he said, "Grief can be all consuming. She walked with me through one of the toughest points in my life, and for that, I will always be grateful to her. So, when the signs started showing up, I ignored them. I didn't want to see. I guess because I needed her; she filled a part of the hole left in my life after Dad died."

Haden took Claire's soft hand and placed it between his two calloused ones. No jolt this time, rather a wave of relief to be close to her. "I want kids, a bunch of them."

∞

Claire recognized the pain she saw in Haden's face, the pain of loss. It bore deep into the lines around his eyes and made him look older. She had walked a long time with a piece of that sharp pain, jabbing at her, keeping her heart raw.

Ryan's leaving had opened up a chasm of fear and self-doubt so big and wide that at first, it had threatened to swallow her whole. For two years, she had asked for a divorce, but he refused. Then last year, Ryan found someone else, and he signed, giving Claire the bridge, she needed to move past the chasm and on to healing.

Now, here she sat, next to a man she hadn't known for more than a few weeks, lost in the comfort he gave. He came when needed. He gave without question. When she turned around, he was there, but would he stay?

Her heart needed to trust he would, but her head screamed she would pay the price.

They were still holding hands when the doctor came into the waiting room. "Mrs. Reed, if you and your husband will step into the room next door, we can talk."

"I'm not…" Claire squeezed his hand.

"Let's go," she said unwilling to go alone.

"Okay." He stood and helped her to her feet, never releasing her hand.

Once in the consulting room, the doctor sat across from them. Claire watched his face for any signs of concern, in order to brace herself.

"Henry is waking up from the anesthesia. He did great."

"What can you tell us about the results?" asked Haden.

"Nothing yet. We should know in a couple of days. How has his stomach been?" asked the doctor.

"Not as bad. He hasn't complained much, but with Henry, you never know. He's not one to complain."

"No, I imagine not." The doctor closed the file. "I'll have the nurse come and get you to take you to the outpatient recovery." He stood. "I'll give you a call in a day or two." He reached out and patted Claire on the shoulder. "Don't worry Mrs. Reed. Henry's tough."

The door closed, and Claire wilted into the chair. "Henry is tough isn't he and brave. You said he was brave."

"Very." Haden reached over and pulled Claire into his arms. "He's going to be okay. No matter the outcome of the test."

She buried her face in his shoulder and let the firmness of his body reassure her.

"Yes, he's going to be all right," she murmured. "He's going to be all right."

The nurse stuck her head in. "If you'll follow me, there's a little man whose anxious to see you two." Grinning, she pointed and asked, "Are you Haden, the guy with the dump truck?"

"Yeah, that's me."

"Well, according to Henry, you're better than sliced bread and chocolate put together."

Haden chuckled. "That's good to know. So, how is he?"

"Talkative, but follow me, and you can see for yourself."

Henry sat up in the bed with Baby beside him. He clutched the baseball glove Haden had given him to his chest, propping his chin on the fingers.

His eyes sparkled, and his voice rose a pitch with excitement when Haden came in behind Claire. “You stayed.”

“Said I would.” Haden rumpled Henry’s hair.

“They gave me apple juice to drink. You want one?”

“No thanks,” they answered together. Claire sat on the side of the bed next to Henry. “We had coffee.”

Henry scrunched his face up. “I like apple juice better.”

Claire’s heart warmed as she and Haden and Henry jabbered on about nothing, telling stupid jokes and making Henry laugh. After about a half hour, Haden pulled out his phone to check the time.

“Listen, I have to go. I need to meet with a foreman about the Wymore place. But I’ll call your mom later and check on you.”

Claire’s pulse skipped a beat. She had hoped he would stay in contact, but there wasn’t anything holding them together. The lie that had been their glue had been dispelled, and in her panic, she had quit her job. Nothing connected them.

Haden rose from the chair. “Can I speak with you for a moment?”

“Sure.” Claire figured he wanted to explain away his act of kindness in the consulting room.

She walked out into the hall.

“I want you to consider coming back to Sawyer Construction. We need you. We can’t find anything, and in a week, we’ll have the office buried in trash again. Jed and Kyle have given me nothing but grief for letting you quit.”

“I don’t know, Haden. There’s still this thing between us. There’s so much I'm not sure of."

"I know, but I'm sure of this, you belong at Sawyer Construction." Claire resisted the urge to lean into him, letting him be her tower of strength. He stood so close. She smelled the musk he wore.

When she looked up into his warm brown eyes, they drew her like magnets closer until she stood on tiptoe and pressed her lips against his.

Catching herself, she stopped but licked her lips to savor his taste. "I'll think about it."

Haden's dimples appeared. "Good."

Chapter Twenty-six

Friday morning had come with a vengeance. Ever since Wednesday, Claire had oscillated between worrying about Henry's results and daydreaming about Haden's kisses. Neither one of them lent much peace to her divided soul.

She pushed the vacuum over the carpet in Henry's room, humming to the song that drifted from her earbuds. Cleaning, she decided would take her mind off both issues. She had donned her red checkered apron and started in Henry's room since he was at Kindergarten.

But apparently, thoughts don't turn off like faucets, and she found herself contemplating Haden's offer.

She needed the work. How else would the stack of medical bills get paid. No Fairy Godmothers for that.

Claire sighed. She replayed that night at the ball field again for the umpteenth time. Why had she let jealousy and fear push her into doing something so stupid. Then, Haden had said she belonged at Sawyer Construction. She found it hard to argue with him when every time he held her, she felt as if she did belong…to him.

And those sweet, delicious kisses. The man had skills.

Claire absent-mindedly shoved the vacuum around, banging into bed posts and chair legs.

When she thought of a relationship with Haden, she always came back to the same heaviness, but she couldn't name it.

She felt as if she were running on a mental hamster wheel. She never got past…What? Her attraction for him? No, that wasn't it.

Frustration filled her. She pushed the vacuum with added force, hitting something under Henry's bed.

Claire leaned over to see what it was, but she couldn't see anything. She didn't need to suck up another dinosaur or miniature truck the crack had eaten. She knew the price of a new vacuum cleaner. This one she intended on guarding.

She knelt down on all fours and ran her hand under the bed. Hitting something soft and squishy, she grabbed a hold of it and dragged it out of its hiding place.

"Awe, Baby, it's you." Claire pulled her headphones off and pushed the pause icon on her phone. Turning Baby over, she gave him a good wiping down with the dusting rag she had tucked in her apron pocket.

She stood to put Baby back in his spot but discovered the baseball glove from Haden occupying the space.

Surprised, she sat down on the side of the bed. Henry adored Haden; there was no question about that. After the dump truck driving, no man would ever compare to Haden Sawyer in Henry's eyes.

She hugged Baby to her. She remembered the day Ryan had bought the dark brown teddy bear at the toy store. He had been so happy about her pregnancy and wanted her to know. When he gave her the gift, a necklace hung from around the bears neck. "A treasure for you and one for the baby." She could almost hear his voice now, saying the words.

Henry clung to the bear because of this story, because it was a connection to a dad he didn't remember.

Claire looked at the glove.

Now, Haden had entered his life. Haden who kept promises and showed up when Henry needed him. When I needed him. Were things changing?

Everything started out rocky with Haden, the traffic jam, the introduction as his girlfriend, the flare ups of her temper, but when he was near or held her hand, or… She closed her eyes. When he kissed her, her heart filled with warmth and tenderness to the point it overwhelmed her.

Perhaps her fears didn't revolve around getting hurt; maybe, she was scared. That was it. She was scared of loving too much.

Had she loved Ryan too much? Did she love Haden too much?

Claire jumped up, clutching the bear. Did she love Haden?

Attraction was one thing, but love? She began to shake.

Startled by the thought and the feelings that accompanied it, she threw the bear onto the bed and stuffed her earphones back into her ears. She turned on the vacuum and turned the music up, trying to drown out the unwelcomed discovery that her heart no longer belonged to her.

∞

Later that afternoon as Claire and Henry came home from the grocery store, Claire's cell phone began vibrating in her back pocket. She dashed for the kitchen and deposited the grocery bags and her purse on the table.

"Henry close the front door for me, please." Claire pulled her phone out and pushed the button.

"Okay, Mom." Henry retraced his steps and pushed the front door closed.

"Hello," Claire answered. She stood listening as Henry unloaded the contents of his lunch bag into the sink.

"Yes, I'm Claire Reed." Again, she paused.

"I've been waiting for your call. Can you tell me the results?" Claire willed herself not to cry if the news was bad.

"You're kidding? No, that's great! I can't believe it."

She listened as the doctor gave her some instructions.

Henry walked over to the table and stood in a chair, unpacking one of the grocery bags.

Once Claire hung up, she reached over and pulled Henry into her arms.

"Mommy, I can't breathe."

"Breathing's overrated. Enjoy the hug."

"Is something wrong?" Henry asked as he wiggled his way out of her arms.

"No, not a thing and nothing's wrong with you either. That was the doctor, and he said the test was clear. He said you're fine. The one thing though is that you can't eat French fries too often."

Henry's face fell. Claire asked, "What's wrong? That's good news."

"No, it's not. That's bad news."

"Why? There are lots of other foods to eat."

"But what am I going to eat with my ketchup?"

Claire rumpled Henry's hair, causing it to poke out all over. "I'm sure we'll find something."

Without giving it a second thought, she scooped up her phone and called Haden. She didn't even wait for him to say hello.

"You're not going to believe this!" she yelled into the phone

"What is it? Is Henry all right? Are you okay?"

"Yes, yes, we're fine. The doctor's office called."

"And…" Haden asked.

"Henry doesn't have Crohn's disease. The doctor thinks he's having problems digesting starches. He said to watch the French fries. Can you believe it. He's fine." Claire plopped down into one of the kitchen chairs. "I can't tell you how relieved I am. It seems like we take one step forward and ten back. It's so nice to get good news for a change."

"That's terrific." Claire heard the relief in Haden's voice. It struck her how much he did care about Henry. He didn't have to be there Wednesday for the GI scopes; he wanted to be there for both of them.

"You're busy," Claire began her excuse to get off the phone, feeling shy now that she had been so open.

"No, I'm not ever too busy for you or Henry."

Claire didn't know what to say. It took her a moment to focus. "Haden, I've been thinking about your offer."

"I tell you what. Why don't we meet tomorrow morning, me, you, and Henry at Aunt Adele's café? We can celebrate Henry's good news in proper style with chocolate chip pancakes, and it'll give us a chance to talk about my offer."

Claire mulled this over for a moment. She knew Henry would love to celebrate his good news with Haden. She couldn't deny him that after being so brave, and now, it was her turn to be brave. "That sounds good. Henry will look forward to it."

"I hope Henry's not the only one." Haden's voice took on a

rumbling timber. Claire blushed as her heart did flip-flops. She had found love when she wasn't looking, a second chance, and she wasn't going to let fear steal it from her.

"Well, I might look forward to it, a little," she teased.

∞

Haden strolled into Adele's a little after eight Saturday morning. He carried a dozen red roses in one arm, and a copy of the Miller Creek Gazette tucked under the other. He spotted Claire and Henry seated near the back in a booth.

He had gone by to see his Aunt Adele and mom the night before to tell them about his plan. He arranged everything with Adele, down to where he wanted her to seat them. She gushed when she heard why he needed her help. His mom had let out a big "Hallelujah" shout, in the excitement.

Adele scooted by him as he headed towards the booth, giving him a wink.

Haden thought his face might break if he smiled any bigger. He had wrestled all week with the loneliness that had invaded his life the minute Claire had evacuated it. But when he saw her at the hospital, he knew. She owned him, heart and soul. Now, he needed her to know it.

Claire broke out into the cutest grin as he neared the table with the roses. "Are those for me?"

"Yes, they are." He handed her the bundle wrapped in green paper. "The new florist said if you put an aspirin in the water, they'll stay fresh longer."

"These are divine, Haden, but what's the occasion?"

"It's to celebrate your return to Sawyer Construction. It's where you belong." Haden slid into the seat across from Claire and Henry.

"Hi Haden. Did you hear? I'm not sick." Henry sat up in his booster chair.

"I sure did, sport." Haden extended his knuckles to Henry for a knuckle bump.

"Do I get something?"

"Henry!" Haden saw Claire's cheeks turn pink. "You don't ask people for gifts. Besides, Haden brought you that awesome baseball glove, remember?"

"For being brave. I remember."

Adele returned with two cups of coffee and a glass of orange juice. "Here are your drinks. Oooh, what beautiful flowers."

"They are nice, aren't they?" Claire beamed.

"Do you want me to put them in a vase for you?"

"Do you have one?" Claire asked.

"Yeah, I can scrounge one up. We keep all kinds of things in the store room for special occasions and such." Adele fished out her order pad and looked at Haden. "Are you guys ready to order?"

"Yes, we all want the chocolate chip pancakes." He looked at Claire to see if she'd let him get away with ordering for all of them.

"That sounds perfect," she said, handing her menu to Adele along with the flowers.

"My favorite!" Henry pumped his arms in the air.

"Mine too," added Haden.

After Adele left, Haden moved the drinks and spread the paper open upside down on the table to page two, so Claire could read it. "I wanted to show you an ad in today's paper. It's part of the reason I wanted to meet you here, so I could show it to you in person."

Claire leaned forward, and Haden pointed to the ad. She read the print in front of her. When she finished, she looked up. "I don't know what to say. This took a great deal of courage to do. Haden I'm so proud of you." Claire reached across the paper and took Haden's hand. Relief washed over him.

"After Sarah let you think that I was the one who didn't want any kids, I got a good taste of my own medicine, and it didn't feel too good. So, after talking it over with Aunt Adele, who gave me the idea of running an ad, I decide I should make things right. After all, there had been around four hundred people who might've gotten the wrong idea."

"Haden!" Claire squeezed his hand, hard.

"I know that's terrible, right? But I wanted a clean slate, so everyone will know that from here on out its nothing but the truth for me. The ad was the answer. It gives Sarah back her good name, and it lets me apologize to her and everyone else." Haden reached out and tapped the ad for emphasis.

This drew Claire's attention to the picture of Jed dancing with his date at the Annual Businessman's Charity Ball at the side of the page. The headline read Henry Reed honored by Local Businessmen's League. He watched as her eyes grew wider, and she jerked the paper towards her to read the article. "Haden, did you have anything to do with this?"

"I may have made the suggestion to Charlie Lee, but it was the board members who voted to donate the money to the Fund-A-Cure foundation in Henry's name. It was one of the few times a motion carried unanimously." He chuckled. "There will also be an amount awarded to Henry as part of a relief fund we've set up to help families with medical needs."

Claire dropped the paper and cupped his hands in both of hers. Admiration radiated from the depths of her vivid green eyes.

Haden hated to break the spell, but he had one last thing to do before Adele arrived with the pancakes. He withdrew his hands from Claire's and leaned his elbows on the table.

Turning his attention to Henry, he said, "Henry, I have something very important I want to discuss with you man to man."

Henry sat straighter in his seat and gave Haden his full attention while he slurped his orange juice.

"Are you ready?"

"Yeah, I'm ready. What is it?" Henry's face grew serious.

Claire narrowed her eyes. "What are you up to Haden?"

"I'm not talking to you. This is between me and Henry. Man talk."

"Sorry, go ahead." Claire held her hands up and leaned back in her seat, amused.

"Now, Henry I need to ask you a question. It's a very important question…" Haden cut his eyes towards Claire to see if she was listening. "I would like your permission to marry your mom."

"You mean be my dad?"

"Yes." He nodded

Before Haden could check to see Claire's reaction, Henry dove across the table and wrapped his arms around his neck. Haden caught the half empty glass of orange juice in one hand while holding onto Henry with the other.

"Oh yes, we want you to marry us, Haden." Henry let go of Haden and stood on the seat of the booth, chanting, "Haden is my daddy. Haden is my daddy."

Haden, undeterred, slid out of the booth and knelt in front of Claire, holding a solitaire diamond ring between his fingers. "What do you say Claire? Will you marry me and let me be Henry's daddy?"

Claire's eyes grew large, and she pressed her lips together, fighting to keep the tears away. "Yes, yes, I will," she answered. "And I know you're the right man for the job."

Before he knew what happened, Claire had pulled him to his feet and wrapped her arms around his waist. Leaning towards her, Haden covered her lips with his, and gently promised to always be there.

When they broke apart, Haden took her small hand in his calloused one and placed the ring on her finger. "I love you, Claire Reed. You've made me the happiest man on the planet."

Grinning, Claire pulled away and went to sit down. "Glad I could help."

But Haden caught her by the arm and pulled her back against him. "Is that all?"

"No, I love you, too and have for a while, I think."

"Good."

Adele came over, grinning so wide you could see the gold filling on her back tooth. "Here is your order, the way you wanted it." She removed the newspaper before placing the plates on the table.

Hugging both of them, Adele said, “I knew you’d work out just fine at the Sawyer Construction Company.”

“How did you know?” asked Claire, playing along as she regained her seat.

“That’s a trade secret.”

“Of nosey matchmakers?” asked Haden.

“No,” said Adele holding her head high. “Of Fairy Godmothers.”

Epilogue

Twelve Weeks Later

The light breeze of fall beckoned them outside on this lazy Sunday evening in September. The wedding shower had lasted until late in the afternoon with most of the town in attendance. Now, they sat in the garden under the big oak tree with its branches, reaching out above them, full of lush green leaves.

Adele sat on the wrought-iron bench next to her sister-in-law Betty. She could tell the party had taken a lot out of her. She still grew tired quickly.

Adele had reassured her that she was as beautiful as ever when her hair had fallen out. But in the last two weeks, it had started to grow back. Stubs of hair peaked through the scarf Betty wore, and Adele thought it was a blessed sight.

Claire, Haden, and Jed sat around in lawn chairs, and Kyle, Daisey, and Henry laid stretched out on a blanket beneath the tree. Everyone was content to listen to the quiet chirping of the cicadas and let the cool breeze lull them into a gentle peace after the rush and activity of the celebration.

"Oh, wait a minute." Kyle popped up, causing Daisey to shift positions. "I almost forgot. I've got one more gift for the groom to be." Adele didn't like the twinkle she saw enter her son's eyes. He was up to something.

Kyle jogged back through the garden and around the side of the house to where the cars were parked. Adele could only guess what he was doing.

"Now, what's this all about?" Haden asked looking at Adele.

"I have no idea. You know how Kyle is. Always got something up his sleeve."

Everyone looked at Daisey. She shrugged.

Kyle soon reappeared around the corner of the house carrying a small box wrapped in wedding paper.

Joining them under the tree, he handed the gift to Haden. "I thought I'd help you keep your word."

Haden's brow's furrowed. "What are you talking about?"

"You know. When you told me that if Claire had any feelings for you, you'd eat Uncle Otis's last cigar."

"What?" Haden sat up straight and shook the box. "You do know I was exaggerating in order to make a point." His gaze met Kyle's.

"You're the one who vowed 'I'm a man of my word from here on out.' Or didn't you mean it?" Kyle grinned, his boyish dimples framing his mouth.

Haden scowled and squirmed in his seat. "I have a feeling I'm going to be eating more than my words."

Adele eyed the box in Haden's hands, trying to figure out what it could be. It was too large to be a cigar box. Surely, Kyle didn't expect Haden to actually eat a cigar.

Claire giggled. "You better open it. Get it over with."

Haden tore the layer of wrapping from the box.

Henry rolled to his knees on the blanket and sat up. "What is it? Is it something for me?" Several guests had brought gifts for Henry as well as for the couple.

Adele called Henry over and let him climb into her lap. They watched as Haden opened the lid of the cardboard box.

Haden's face lit up. Relief washed over Adele. She never knew what to expect from her son when a wild idea got a hold of him.

Claire leaned over the arm of her lawn chair and held the box for Haden as he lifted out a small glass top humidor that contained the last of Otis Sawyer's cigars. "You preserved it." Adele could hear the tenderness in Haden's voice.

"What a wonderful idea." Adele's heart swelled with pride.

Kyle winked at his mom. "I couldn't let a lug like Haden eat it."

Everybody chuckled. "Instead, I asked Aunt Betty if I could buy this humidor for it. It needed to be put in moisture, or it would've dried out and rotted. I wanted it to be something special, and I thought this way, we'd always have a part of Uncle Otis with us."

"How thoughtful," said Claire, her voice cracking.

"What's in the box?" asked Henry, straining against Adele's arms to see. Haden stood and patted his younger cousin on the shoulder, "Thanks, man." Then walked over to Henry.

"A cigar." Haden answered, leaning down to show Henry what was in the box.

"I want a cigar." Henry cried.

"You're too young." Adele gave him a squeeze. "Wait a few years." Henry wiggled free and moved to Betty's lap.

“Maybe, I can help.” Haden handed the humidor to Adele and reached toward Claire who handed him a white plastic bag, from which he pulled eight blue bubble gum cigars. “I'd like to make an announcement please.”

“Another one? Didn't you make enough speeches and announcements for one day?” asked Jed who had his legs stretched out in front of him and his head resting on the back of the lawn chair.

Haden turned towards him. “No, and this one is important, so listen up.”

Claire stood and moved to stand by Haden. She took his hand in hers. “I'm officially announcing Betty Sawyer is expecting a grandson, a one soon-to-be Henry Sawyer.”

“Henry Sawyer? Don't you mean Henry Reed?” asked Betty who was now holding Henry on her lap. Adele smiled as she caught Betty snuggling Henry close to her.

“No, once we're married in December, we're going to start the adoption process. Henry will become a full fledge Sawyer.” Adele squealed, clapping her hands while Betty squeezed poor Henry till he nearly lost his breath.

“Your Dad would be so proud of the fine young men you've all turned out to be. And Henry would've been the icing on the cake.” Betty beamed.

Haden handed out the cigars. When he got to Henry, he asked, “What do you think Henry? Do you want to be a Sawyer?”

Henry took the bubble gum cigar from Haden's hand. He sat looking at it for a minute. When he looked up, he wore a stern expression for a five-year-old. "Do Sawyers get cigars?"

"Yes, but only candy ones till they're grown." Haden answered.

"Do they drive big trucks?"

"Yes." Jed chuckled. "That's one of the things we do best."

"Do they play baseball?"

"Yes." The three men answered in unison. Kyle added, "Sawyers are great at baseball."

"And not bad at coaching either." Haden added.

"Then I want to be a Sawyer." Henry slid off Betty's lap and buried his face in Haden's shirt, throwing his arms as far around the man as they could reach. Haden lean forward and engulfed the small boy in his arms.

Adele's heart melted at the sight of her family. Now, if only the other two were married…

The End

Dear Friends,

Thank you for joining me in this adventure with Claire and Haden and the Sawyer Family.

They are like so many of us with our ups and downs, and day to day struggles. We too often feel abandoned and isolated when we are up against the hard places in life like Claire and Super Henry with his illness of Juvenile Dermatomyositis or Betty with her cancer.

Too many times these days, we think our struggle is ours and ours alone. But dear friend, I would encourage you that as God's children we never walk alone.

My hope is that this snapshot of the Sawyer family encourages you in your own struggles. Just as Haden and Claire found loves blessing and grace, I know that God's love will shed His grace and blessing on you.

God's Best,
Bonita Y. McCoy

About the Author

Bonita Y. McCoy hails from the Great State of Alabama where she lives on a five-acre farm with two horses, two dogs, two cats, and one husband who she's had for over twenty-eight years.

She is a mother to three mostly grown sons and two beautiful daughters-in-law, one who joined the family from Japan. She loves God, and she loves to write. Her blogs and stories are an expression of both these passions.

She is an active member of the American Christian Fiction Writers, Huntsville Writers Group, and North Alabama Christian Writers. She contributes to the blog Inspired Prompts.

You can catch up with Bonita online:

www.bonitaymccoy.com
www.facebook.com/bonita.mccoy
www.instagram.com/bonitaymccoy

Or catch her blogs:

www.courageouswriters.com
www.beautifulpiecesofgrace.blogspot.com

Coming Soon ….

Perfect Timing
A Sawyer Family Novel

Jed Sawyer made his way down the sidewalk on Main Street his mind on the construction job his company was scheduled to start in the next week. Between the issues at the Wymore Hotel site, the new job, and his brother's upcoming wedding, he didn't think he'd have any time to work at the Miller Creek Rescue Mission over the holidays.

What did it matter? He kicked a rock from the sidewalk and watched it skitter across the black pavement.

He preferred his time be eaten away with busyness. It kept his mind off of other things like his Aunt Adele and her failed attempts at matchmaking. She'd set him up with half the single women in town, most of whom he'd known since childhood, but it hadn't worked out.

No chemistry. Just a lot of polite conversation. "How's your mom. Saw your brother last week," followed by a sweet smile and a call me.

But he never did. He'd been on more first dates in the last month than his entire 32 years of existence. The women of the town had dubbed him the "one time only" special.

The only advice his dear aunt had given him, "You can't rush these things."

No, but eventually, they would run out of women in Miller Creek…And he had no intentions of going global.

Fall 2019

83916215R00161

Made in the USA
San Bernardino, CA
01 August 2018